She'd come to a halt, pausing in front of a small detached bungalow in a leafy avenue just around the corner from his rented house.

'This is me,' she said, and he opened the garden gate and walked her to the door. The porch light wasn't on and the area was shaded from the streetlight by a tree, creating an intimate little space.

Too intimate.

Suddenly the air was filled with tension, crackling with electricity, heavy with expectation and suppressed emotion. His? Hers?

Both?

He couldn't kiss her. It would be crazy. They were colleagues. He'd told his grandmother that. Hell, he'd told Kate that, and he didn't want to muddy the waters at work.

But he wanted to kiss her.

Despite all his best intentions, despite the serious talking-to he'd given himself the night before, he wanted to kiss her.

And she wanted to kiss him. He could feel it in the tension coming off her in waves, in the hesitation, the breathless sense of anticipation…

Dear Reader

We always think *It'll never happen to me*—but sometimes, of course, it does. Because 'it' always has to happen to someone. And of all the things to happen an inherited disorder is probably one of the most insidious. From the moment of diagnosis in a family member the threat of potentially developing the condition, whatever it might be, hangs over those who are possibly afflicted with the defective gene—and the fallout of this emotional minefield can be devastating.

Ed is in this position, and the decision to have the genetic screening test and find out the result can only be his. But no man is an island, no matter how hard he might try to isolate himself from the love and concern of those around him. He's doing OK, though, he thinks—and then he meets Annie and everything changes.

This is the story of a man who's made some tough decisions, who's never ducked out of his responsibilities or taken the easy route, and the woman who loves him enough to help him through the hardest step of all, whatever the outcome. I give them to you with my love. Take care of them. They're very special to me.

Caroline

RISK OF A LIFETIME

BY
CARLINE ANDERSON

Published in Great Britain 2014
by Mills & Boon, an imprint of Harlequin (UK) Limited,
Large Print edition 2014
Eton House, 18-24 Paradise Road,
Richmond, Surrey, TW9 1SR

ISBN: 978-0-263-23897-6

Harlequin (UK) Limited's policy is to use papers that are natural, renewable and recyclable products and made from wood grown in sustainable forests. The logging and manufacturing processes conform to the legal environmental regulations of the country of origin.

Printed and bound in Great Britain
by CPI Antony Rowe, Chippenham, Wiltshire

Caroline Anderson has the mind of a butterfly. She's been a nurse, a secretary, a teacher, run her own soft furnishing business, and now she's settled on writing. She says, 'I was looking for that elusive something. I finally realised it was variety, and now I have it in abundance. Every book brings new horizons and new friends, and in between books I have learned to be a juggler. My teacher husband, John, and I have two beautiful and talented daughters, Sarah and Hannah, umpteen pets, and several acres of Suffolk that nature tries to reclaim every time we turn our backs!'

Recent titles by Caroline Anderson:

Mills & Boon® Medical Romance™

THE SECRET IN HIS HEART
FROM CHRISTMAS TO ETERNITY
THE FIANCÉE HE CAN'T FORGET*
TEMPTED BY DR DAISY*
ST PIRAN'S: THE WEDDING OF THE YEAR†
THE SURGEON'S MIRACLE

**The Legendary Walker Doctors*
†*St Piran's Hospital*

Mills & Boon® Cherish™

SNOWED IN WITH THE BILLIONAIRE
THE VALTIERI BABY
VALTIERI'S BRIDE
THE BABY SWAP MIRACLE
MOTHER OF THE BRIDE

These books are also available in eBook format from www.millsandboon.co.uk

DEDICATION

For my fellow MedRom authors, an incredible support group of amazingly talented women who never fail to say the right thing or tell me what I need to know.
Girls, you rock!

**Praise for
Caroline Anderson:**

'…an engrossing, enthralling and highly enjoyable tale that will move you to tears and keep you riveted… Moving, heartbreaking and absolutely fantastic, with WEDDING OF THE YEAR Caroline Anderson is at her mesmerising best!'
—*www.cataromance.com* on
ST PIRAN'S: WEDDING OF THE YEAR

'This lovely reunion romance is rich with emotion and humour, and all of the characters are exquisitely rendered.'
—*RT Book Reviews* on
MOTHER OF THE BRIDE

CHAPTER ONE

'OH, MY…'

'What?'

Annie looked up at Kate, registered the slack jaw and widening eyes, and started to turn her head.

'Don't look!' Kate hissed, dragging her eyes back to the notes.

'Don't look at what?'

'Total hottie heading this way. Absolute classic TDH. He can't possibly be our new SpR, we don't get that lucky.' Her eyes flicked up again briefly. 'OMG, he is *gorgeous*! I think I'm in love.'

She fanned herself theatrically with the notes, and Annie chuckled. *TDH*? *OMG*? 'You can't possibly be in love—'

'You wanna bet?' Kate sneaked another peek and her voice shifted up an octave. 'He's coming in! And he's got a stethoscope round his neck…!'

Annie rolled her eyes and snatched the notes from her, just as the door behind her swung open.

'Hi. I heard the paeds trauma call. Want any help?'

Well, she had to look now. Apart from the fact that he was talking to them, that voice was—well, compelling went a short way towards describing it. Dark, molten chocolate, with a tiny kick of chilli that left a lingering warmth in its wake.

There was no way his body could match that voice. She turned her head, smile at the ready, and her breath hitched.

The voice didn't do him justice.

Neither had Kate, but then she'd been virtually incoherent. She'd been right to a point, though. Tall, dark and handsome for sure—and, yes, completely and utterly gorgeous, if you were into that type, but she wasn't. Not that she had a type any more, but if she did, it wouldn't be a man like this.

At all.

Broad, lean, toned, reeking of testosterone overlaid with fresh air and sunshine, everything about him screamed trouble! His slate-blue bedroom eyes were fringed with black lashes a mile long, and that lazy stride ate up the floor as he advanced towards them.

Her first instinct was to run, but then common sense intervened. He was a doctor, apparently, possibly their new registrar, and he was offering to help, and that made him *definitely* her type. The mind-numbingly gorgeous packaging didn't matter. What mattered was that he was here, on a day when their staffing levels were stretched to the limit, and frankly if he'd had two heads she'd welcome him with open arms. But—sheesh. Did he have to be *quite* so luscious?

She resisted the urge to fan herself with the notes *à la* Kate and found her voice from somewhere.

'Maybe. Don't know much about it yet. Child versus car, possible head injury, but that's all we have as yet. ETA any second.'

She stuck out her hand to him, determined to behave like a grown-up and not a hormonal teenager, and tilted her head way back to meet his eyes. 'I'm Annie Brooks, by the way,' she said, proud of her voice for not coming out like a demented squeak. 'I'm job-sharing with Andy Gallagher. And you are...?'

'Ah. Sorry. Ed Shackleton, James Slater's new specialist registrar,' he confirmed, those heavily lashed eyes the colour of storm clouds meeting hers and holding them. A warm, strong hand engulfed her own as that firm, chiselled mouth tilted into a smile, and everything inside her lurched.

Her pulse spiked, and she could feel heat spreading out from her hand, all the way up her arm, settling in the region of her locked-down diaphragm like a fireball.

And she was blushing.

No. Not a blush. A flush.

Different.

Worse, the heat from the fireball was spreading upwards now, creeping up her body towards her face.

Could he see it? Please, God, no—

Breathe, Annie!

The sound of the siren penetrated the swirling fog that was her brain, and she sucked in a breath and snatched her hand back, resisting the urge to wipe it on her scrubs, as if she could wipe away her reaction to his touch.

'Sounds like we might be in business. Are we ready?'

One look at Kate and it was clear that she was. Ready for anything their new SpR cared to throw at them—unlike her. She was blushing and flushing and generally getting in a dither. Oh, this was ridiculous…

But Kate's sensible self was back in charge, thank goodness, and she nodded briskly. 'We're good to go.'

'Right.'

The sirens screamed to a halt, leaving a shocking silence, and her brain finally snapped back to life.

'OK, we're on. Let's go and find out what we've got.'

'Mind if I tag along?' he asked quietly. 'I'm Paeds trained.'

'Sure. Feel free. We can always use another pair of hands.'

She pushed the door out of the way, oddly

desperate to escape the confines of Resus. She didn't *do* this—didn't get hot and flustered and all quivery inside.

Ever. At all. Men were firmly off her menu, now and into the hereafter. Maybe longer.

And Dr Gorgeous was definitely a man.

She took a deep breath and walked briskly out to the ambulance bay, deeply conscious of the man keeping pace by her side. The doors of the ambulance flew open, the steps flipped down and the doctor in her kicked in.

At last.

She forgot all about him, forgot everything except the sobbing child and the look of terror on the face of his mother as the paramedics who'd brought them in reeled off his stats and the treatment to date.

And as she nodded at the paramedic and smiled at the mother, she could see Ed scanning the child with his eyes, assessing him rapidly. Good. She turned her attention to the mother.

'Hi, I'm Annie, I'm a doctor, and this is Ed. We're going to be looking after your son. What's his name?'

'Cody,' his mother said unsteadily. 'Cody Phillips. Oh, please, help him.'

'We will.'

The calm, confident voice came from Ed, who was leaning over the trolley as they pushed it in, looking down at the boy. Cody's right eye was swollen shut, a blue stain under the skin of his temple and cheek, and he was sobbing, but Ed just smiled and held his hand as if it was all fine. 'Hi, Cody, I'm Ed. It's all right, you're in good hands. We've got you, mate. We'll soon make you feel better.'

The low, quiet voice was reassuring, and Annie felt the tension drain out of her. Kind as well as gorgeous. Now to check out his clinical skills to see if they matched up. He was certainly doing all right so far.

'You can lead if you like,' she said, and he nodded.

'Will you do the FAST scan, please?'

'Sure.'

Like a well-oiled machine, the team went into action, and gradually Annie felt herself relax.

He was good, she realised. More than that, he

was very good. She stopped watching his every move, and concentrated on what she was doing.

'Results are through.'

'And?'

He moved up behind her, so close she could feel the warmth coming off him. She forced herself to focus on the screen.

'Well, according to the report he's got no obvious brain injury and there certainly doesn't seem to be any sign of it, but he's got a fracture of the right orbit.'

Ed was looking over her shoulder at the MRI scan images, his head just in her line of sight, and he winced. 'Must have been quite a whack. I wonder if he'll end up with any loss of vision. The swelling could put a lot of pressure on that eye.' He leaned in closer, bringing him right up against her. 'Am I imagining it, or is the orbit slightly compressed?'

She shifted sideways a fraction. 'Possibly. What a shame. Poor little Cody.'

She turned but Ed was still right there, studying the images on the screen, his chest just inches from her nose. She sucked in a breath, but that was a mistake, because with the air came a faint trace of soap and red-blooded man.

'Want me to talk to the parents?' he asked, the tingle of chilli in that low, melting-chocolate voice setting fire to her nerve endings again.

'No, I'll do it,' she said briskly.

She ducked past him, and he followed her back to the child's side where Cody's parents were waiting anxiously for the verdict, his mother's eyes brimming with fear as she watched them approach.

It wasn't surprising. Cody's father had arrived shortly after the ambulance, and although they'd eliminated any other injuries in the last hour, this was the thing that was worrying them all the most and frankly this family needed some good news. Annie smiled at them reassuringly.

'OK, we've had a look at the report now and although he's got a facial fracture Cody doesn't have an obvious brain injury, which is great news—'

'So—he's all right?' his mother asked, hope replacing the fear.

'Well, nothing obvious has been detected in his brain,' she cautioned, 'but that doesn't mean he's out of the woods yet. He'll be a bit concussed and have a horrible headache anyway, but sometimes the brain swells after a bump like this so he'll need constant monitoring for the next few hours just in case, but they should be able to manage it if it happens. However, the fracture extends to his eye socket where his cheekbone's taken the impact, so he's certainly not unscathed. It's going to be sore and because of where it is, it might have implications for his sight.'

Her eyes widened, the fear back. A new fear this time, and she pressed her fingers to her mouth.

'He could go blind?' the father asked, his voice rough with emotion.

'I think that's unlikely, but it might alter his vision in that eye. They'll get the ophthalmic and maxillo-facial teams to have a really good look at it while he's in here, but it might take time for the swelling to go down before they can assess it fully. As soon as they have a bed he'll be transferred up to the paediatric intensive care unit, PICU, for monitoring and pain relief until they're happy with him, and then he'll be moved to a ward. They'll talk to you up there about his progress and what they're going to do, if anything. He'll probably be in here a couple of days, all being well, but so far we're cautiously optimistic that he'll make a full recovery. Children are very resilient.'

His mother's shoulders slumped—with relief? Worry? Guilt?

All of it. She knew all about a mother's guilt. She lived with it every working day, but needs must and so far the girls seemed well adjusted.

Which was more than she could say for herself at the moment. She'd just caught another whiff of Ed Shackleton's special blend of soap and pheromones, and she had to force herself to concentrate on talking to Cody's parents.

'I'll chase up PICU,' Kate was saying, and she nodded.

'Thanks. Right, I'm just going to update the notes, and as soon as they've got a bed free, we'll be moving him. You'll be able to stay with him overnight.'

His mother nodded, and Annie stepped away from them, grabbed the notes and moved to the side to write them up.

Behind her she could hear Ed's voice murmuring to the parents, answering their endless questions with sensibly noncommittal answers.

He'd been amazing. Calm, steady, gentle, soothing the distressed child with a competence that usually came with years of practice.

He was probably a father. Almost inevitably. Someone was bound to have snapped him up, he was far too good to be on the shelf.

Unless he was a player, but he didn't seem the type. Far too wholesome and straightforward. Until the lights went out?

It was none of her business, she reminded herself crossly. And in any case she wasn't interested.

At all!

So this was Annie Brooks.

He glanced across at her, writing up the notes

while Kate kept an eye on Cody's monitor and pottered quietly in the background.

Her back was to him, which meant he could study her without detection. She wasn't short, but she certainly wasn't tall. Her head would tuck easily under his chin. And her body was—well, just a body. Nothing out of the ordinary. She wasn't fat, she wasn't thin, she was just… womanly, he thought with interest. Feminine. Her curves were in all the right places, and she moved with grace.

Except when she was rattled. Then she moved awkwardly, self-consciously. He found that interesting, too.

Her mid-brown hair was twisted up in a clip at the back, out of the way. A strand had escaped, and she was fiddling with it, one finger twirling the little curl round and round.

It was a curiously innocent gesture, utterly unconscious, the sort of thing people did when they were concentrating hard, and he found it strangely touching.

James had told him about her. He'd said she was competent, kind and easy to work with, but he was sure that underneath the surface there was much, much more to her than that.

Unlike Kate.

There were hundreds of girls like Kate, nice girls, pretty girls, girls who made it clear with every glance that they were available, but Annie…

Annie intrigued him. For a moment there, right at the beginning, he'd had his doubts about her. She'd seemed ruffled by his arrival, somehow, distracted and unfocused, but then the ambulance had arrived and she'd changed.

It was as if she'd engaged a different gear, and it had all settled down. She'd become everything that James had told him she was, and he began to think he'd imagined that sizzle of awareness.

Until their glances had met again. For a fleeting moment the forget-me-not blue of her eyes had locked with his, and then it had been back, whatever 'it' was. Some crazy pull between them, like kissing dolls, the magnetic attraction drawing them inexorably together.

And she seemed to resent it, to pull back from it as if it was unwelcome, turning her head and carrying on as if nothing had happened, but it had, and she'd dismissed it.

He felt a twinge of regret. A little light relief to take his mind off the coming months of family trauma and upheaval might have been welcome, but it probably wasn't sensible. He had nothing to offer, he wasn't here for long and anyway it was never a good idea to muddy the waters with someone you worked with.

Kate, for instance. She'd made it blindingly obvious she was up for anything he might suggest, but anyway, even if he found her attractive, which he didn't except in the most superficial and basic way, the same principle applied—

'PICU are ready for him.'

He nodded at Kate and switched his eyes to Annie.

'Annie?'

'All done. Kate, will you go with him, please?'

She slapped the notes shut, put them on the trolley, shook hands with the parents and the two of them watched as Cody was whisked away.

'Poor little boy. He's going to have a cracking headache for a few days,' he said softly.

Annie nodded. 'Let's hope that's all. Good teamwork, by the way. Thank you.'

'My pleasure. Thank you for letting me join you.'

Annie flashed him a quick acknowledging glance, the first time she'd met his eyes for a while now. Well, since *that* time, when he'd felt that sizzle of awareness again.

But there was no awareness now that he could see, and her voice was brisk and businesslike.

'You're welcome. It's nice to know we've got someone on the team with Paeds training. You can never have too many. Right, I need to go and chase up some tests,' she said, and he could have sworn she was running away.

From him? Surely not. He hadn't given her any reason to feel threatened or harassed in any way.

So why was he so much of a threat to her?

'Hello, my darlings! How are you?'

'Mummy!'

The girls ran to her, hugging her in stereo, dragging her to the table to see what they were doing.

'We've made you a picture!'

'I did this bit, and Chloe did that bit—'

'And Grace put the ears on the bunny, and MamaJo let us eat the last chocolate bunny!'

'Did she?' Annie laughed at her mother and shook her head. 'I thought we didn't eat chocolate between meals?'

'But we had it for pudding!' Grace told her solemnly. 'MamaJo didn't cheat.'

Annie bit the inside of her cheek to stop herself laughing. 'I'm glad to hear it. And it's a lovely picture. Thank you. As soon as it's dry, we'll put it up on the wall. Now, how about your bath, and then I'll read you a story.'

'I want to choose—'

'No, it's my turn—'

'I'm choosing,' she said firmly. 'I think it's my turn. How about Peter Rabbit?'

'Yes!'

They ran for the bathroom, and she rolled her eyes at her mother. 'Don't worry about the mess, I'll clear it up,' she promised, and followed them.

Chloe, always the one in trouble, was diving headfirst over the side of the bath, trying to put the plug in, and she fished her back out, put the plug in and turned on the taps.

'So what else have you done today?' she asked, quickly stripping their clothes off and throwing them at the laundry basket.

She bathed them while they chattered, washing their hair—Grace's angelic pale blonde curls, Chloe's wildly tangled chocolate-brown mop—and then combed it through with conditioner, rinsed and blotted and fished them out of the bath to finish drying while the water drained out.

And all the time they were talking, telling her about their day, their friends, the helpers at the nursery, and amidst the lively chatter Annie felt herself starting to relax.

'Gosh, we've all had a busy day. Come on, let's go and snuggle up and have a story, and then it's time for bed.'

She settled them down, tidied up the bathroom and went back to the kitchen.

'Oh, Mum, I said I'd clear up.'

'You've done enough, you've been at work.

Here, I've made you tea. Come and sit down and tell me about your day.'

Annie flopped into the corner of the sofa and sighed. 'It was exhausting. We've had one thing after another. I don't think I've sat down for more than a few minutes all day. How were the girls? They seem lively enough.'

'Fine. No problem. They really seem to like the hospital nursery. They were full of everything they'd done today.'

'I noticed,' she said drily. 'They didn't stop telling me about it all through their bath, but at least it's a good sign.'

It *was* good. More than good. It was essential. Her mother was wonderful, and she couldn't possibly have managed without her since the twins had been born, but she felt so guilty asking, so guilty burdening her with the girls. Although she'd said a million times that having her granddaughters wasn't a burden, she knew it was. It had to be. They were a burden on *her*, and she was their mother, although if she had her time over again she'd change nothing. Well, except their father, who'd had the fastest pair of running shoes she'd ever seen, but that wasn't their fault.

Chloe and Grace were the most wonderful things that had ever happened to her, and the fact that they were happy at the nursery was important for all of them. If the girls weren't happy, none of them would be happy.

'How's Grannie?' she asked, and her mother shrugged.

'Oh, much the same. Stubborn, independent, won't take any painkillers and then wonders why everything hurts.'

Annie smiled ruefully at her mother. 'Are you OK, Mum? I know you say we aren't a burden, but between my girls and your mother, you're stuck between a rock and a hard place.'

'No, I'm not.' Her mother brushed it aside with a dismissive flap of her hand. 'What else would I be doing with my time? Arranging flowers in the church? Working in a charity shop?'

She got to her feet, the subject closed. 'Are you ready for your supper? It's Thai curry. I'll just heat it up and we can eat it in here in front of the television, with your feet up.'

Annie smiled gratefully at her. 'That sounds lovely. I'm starving. I haven't eaten all day. Well, only chocolate biscuits.'

Her mother tutted and walked off in the direction of the kitchen, and she watched her go and felt guilt. Always guilt.

She should have got up, gone to help, but she was exhausted. It had been a killer shift, not made any easier by trying to dodge Ed Shackleton. Impossible. They'd seemed to end up working together all day.

Which was fine. Working with him was fine. He was great to work with. It was those little moments in between, when the pressure was off and he'd strip off his gloves and apron and fold his arms and slouch back against the wall with that casual grace…

She rested her head back, gave a little sigh and closed her eyes, but there he was, welded on to her retinas—laughing at something silly, sprinting to the ambulance bay, snapping into action when someone had arrested in Resus—images of him tormented her and she sat forward and dropped her head into her hands.

'What's up?'

'Oh, nothing. New colleague. He's a bit…'

'Useless?'

'Oh, no, he's not useless. Far from it. He's excellent. He's just—I don't know. *There*. All the time.'

What was it with a mother's radar? She could almost hear the antenna twirling.

'Single?'

She stuck the fork into her curry and lifted a chunk of chicken up to her mouth.

'Mum, I have no idea. It's irrelevant. I'm not interested.'

'How old?'

She shrugged. 'I don't know. Thirty? Thirty-two? He's a registrar.'

And he didn't wear a ring, which meant nothing, of course, because she didn't either and she was far from free. Single, yes, but free? Available? Not in this lifetime.

'So what's the problem with him?'

Nothing she was about to discuss with her mother!

'Nothing. There's no problem. It's just—settling into a new working relationship. It's difficult.'

Which was a downright lie, because there was nothing difficult about it. Not professionally. They seemed to work together seamlessly as if they'd done it for years, anticipating each other, communicating without words.

They made a great team.

She just didn't want to be on the same team as a man like Ed Shackleton, because he played havoc with her hard-won peace of mind, and she resented that.

A lot.

Ed let himself in and closed the door softly, following the sound of running water to the kitchen.

'Hi, Marnie. How're you doing?'

His grandmother dried her hands and smiled fondly at him. 'All the better for seeing you. How was your first day?'

He laughed softly and hugged her. 'It was fine. Nice people, interesting cases. How's Grumps?'

She shrugged, and he saw the shimmer of tears

in her eyes. 'Oh, bit up and down today. You know. Living up to his name.'

He knew only too well, and he hugged her again, rocking her against his chest as she'd rocked him so many, many times over the years.

She let him hold her for a while, then sighed softly and pushed away, her hands, the hands that so many times had wiped away his childish tears, gentle on his chest. He let her go, tipped up her chin and stared down into her eyes. Her own tears now weren't very far away, and he frowned and tutted softly.

'I'm here for you, Marnie, you know that, don't you? Any time, day or night. You just have to call me.'

'I know that, darling. Thank you.'

He shook his head. 'Don't thank me. We're all in this together. I love him, too, you know.'

'I know.' She sighed. 'I think he's going to need a wash and a change before we settle him for the night.'

'OK. I'll sort him out. You make yourself a drink and sit down and have a rest. You look done in.'

It took him a while to sort out his grandfather. It wasn't helped by the fact that the old man was a bit feisty and resistant to his physio.

But when Ed tucked him back up in bed, settled him on his pillows and kissed him goodnight, the old man settled back with a sigh.

'That's better, Edward.'

The words were slurred, but he knew what his grandfather was saying and it was the nearest he'd get to thanks. His answering smile was a little crooked. 'We aim to please, Grumps.'

'Well, go on. All done now.'

Ed sighed and straightened up, the tenuous link broken. 'Goodnight, Grumps. Sleep well. I'll see you in the morning.'

There was a grunt, but the old man was already drifting off, and he went out and closed the door softly behind him.

His grandmother was waiting in the kitchen, a cup by the kettle. 'Tea or coffee?'

'Oh, tea, weak. I've had too much coffee today.'

'So how was he with you?'

'OK. Bit argumentative.' He gave a wry grin, and his grandmother smiled sadly.

'I don't know what we'd do without you.' Her face crumpled briefly. 'Hideous bloody disease,' she muttered, a little quiver in her voice. 'It's so cruel, so wicked. He used to be such a nice man, so kind and affectionate, just like you. I can't bear the thought of having to watch you disintegrate like him—'

'You won't have to,' he said firmly. 'I've told you that.'

'So you have,' she said quietly, and then she straightened up and looked him in the eye with that way of hers that told him she knew he was lying.

He felt a flicker of guilt and dismissed it. It wasn't really a lie. She wouldn't see him deteriorate like his grandfather—but possibly only because she was unlikely to live long enough for the disease to manifest itself. If he'd even got the gene…

He drank his tea, chatted about his day to give his grandmother something to distract her from the topic he was so keen to avoid, and then left her, driving the short distance to his rented house.

He hadn't needed to rent it. He could have stayed with his grandparents or his parents. Both of them lived within minutes of the hospital, but this had been closer, and he'd used that as an excuse because he'd needed it. It was his sanctuary, his private space, his bolthole from the awful reality that was his potential destiny.

He parked in the carport at the back of the garden and let himself in through the conservatory. It was a lovely evening, a little chilly but he didn't mind that. He needed the fresh air. He poured himself a glass of wine, took it back out to the garden and dropped into the swing seat, shifting it idly to and fro with one foot and letting his mind drift over the day.

And centre stage was Annie Brooks.

She was older than him. Mid-thirties? Maybe late? He didn't know exactly, but she was consultant grade and even with his rigid focus on his career he hadn't got there yet. Just this last rung on the ladder to go and he'd be able to look for a consultant's post.

Where would he be then?

London? Back to Great Ormond Street, maybe.

Not here, that was for sure. Once his grandfather had gone, there would be nothing to keep him here in this quiet coastal backwater where nothing much ever happened.

At least, it hadn't in the last thirty-two years, and he had no reason to believe it would happen now just because he'd come home to watch his grandfather die a slow and lingering death.

He sighed, the image of his grandmother's face as she'd looked at him in the kitchen triggering another twinge of guilt.

Did she really know he was lying?

He hadn't lied, though. Not exactly, and she wouldn't have to watch him disintegrate, not unless he got really unlucky. He'd told her he hadn't had a positive result from the predictive screening test, which was true, because he hadn't had the result at all.

He'd had the genetic counselling, the blood test, gone through the whole process right up to the bitter end. But he hadn't taken that last step of hearing his fate, and he didn't want to. It was his life. He could make his own decisions about it, and choosing whether or not to know the truth about his own destiny was one of them. Not telling his family about that decision was another, but it *would* stop with him, that wasn't a lie, because he wasn't having children.

Ever.

And nor was he taking some poor unsuspecting woman with him on the journey to hell, if that should turn out to be his fate.

His grandmother's face disappeared, replaced inexplicably by the face of Annie Brooks, and he frowned.

No. No way. He wasn't touching her with a bargepole. She was too nice, too decent for the only kind of relationship he had in mind. He'd be better off with Kate. At least she knew the rules.

Except he didn't want Kate.

He wanted Annie, and he couldn't have her. It wasn't fair to her. And anyway, she'd made it clear she wanted to put as much distance as possible between them at all times.

Well, thank goodness one of them had some common sense.

He swore softly, drained the wine and went to bed.

CHAPTER TWO

THERE WAS SOMETHING different about him the next day.

Annie couldn't put her finger on it, and it took her till lunchtime to work out what it was.

He was avoiding her eye.

It had taken her that long to cotton on because she'd been so busy avoiding his, but once she realised it, she felt curiously, stupidly disappointed.

Why? She didn't *want* him to look at her, to crowd her space, to be underfoot all the time like he had been yesterday.

Did she?

No!

'Annie?'

She glanced up to see James Slater, their clinical lead, standing a few feet away, watching her with his head tilted to one side.

'Oh. Hi.' She smiled apologetically at him.

'Sorry, I was miles away. What can I do for you, James?'

'Nothing. Absolutely nothing, so why don't you take lunch now while it's so quiet?'

'Shh.' She pressed her finger to her lips, and he chuckled.

'Superstitious?'

She grinned. 'Always. But I will grab some lunch while the going's good. We didn't have time yesterday, in case you're running away with the idea that we had an idle day!'

'No, I gather it was chaos. Sorry I had to bail on you for that meeting. How was Ed?'

Too beautiful for his own good. Or hers.

'Good. Great. Excellent doctor.'

'I'm glad about that. I thought he would be. His references were stunning and we were really lucky to get him. Right, off you go before that damn phone rings.'

She grinned again, saluted and went, grabbing her bag from her locker on the way, then hurried outside to go round to the café in the sunshine.

And bumped straight into Ed.

Literally.

'Aagh!'

She leapt back, clutching at her scrub top and pulling it hastily away from her chest. 'Sheesh, that's hot!' she gasped, flapping the fabric to cool it as the coffee soaked straight through and drenched her.

'Hell, Annie, I'm sorry. Are you all right?'

He was shaking cappuccino froth off his hand, and she tilted her head and gave him a sarky look. 'Oh, peachy—apart from being doused in scalding coffee! Why didn't you have a lid on it?'

'I did—you squashed it when you ran into it. I'm so sorry. Are you all right? You're not really scalded, are you?'

She thought about it and shook her head. Her bra was sopping, and the coffee had been hot but not hot enough to damage her. She could feel it cooling down already in the light breeze.

'Don't worry, I won't sue you. I'm just going to be wringing wet and a little fragrant for the rest of the day,' she said wryly.

'Yeah, you probably need to change.'

'Really? I thought I'd wander round like this

all day wearing cappuccino—set a new trend, you know?'

'You don't have to be sarcastic—'

'I can be what I like, I'm the one soaked to the skin with it,' she retorted, but then she gave a despairing laugh and shook her head. 'Don't worry, I can find myself some new scrubs. The underwear might be harder.'

'Ah. Sorry, I can't help you there. I don't have my spare bra in my locker today.'

She looked up, a surprised laugh on her lips, and their eyes met and locked, the laughter dying as heat flared between them.

Why were they even talking about her underwear?

She dragged her eyes away. 'Look, it's fine. I'm sorry about the coffee, I'll get you another one while I'm in the café.'

'Forget it. I'll get myself another one. Look, why don't you go and change and we'll go over there together and I'll buy you lunch?'

'Do you have time?'

That wasn't what she'd meant to say! No, no, no! She should have told him it wasn't necessary and she'd rather be alone!

Her mouth, however, didn't seem to be under her control any more, and he cornered her with his next words.

'I've got time. I wasn't going to bother to eat, but as it's quiet—'

'Shush! What is it with everyone today?'

He grinned, his mouth kicking up on one side, and she felt her insides turn over.

'Go on, hurry up, get changed and we'll grab a sandwich and eat it in the park. Shoo.'

She must be mad.

She dabbed the coffee out of her bra—thankfully not a moulded-cup T-shirt bra but just a thin lace one—squashed it dry with paper towels, then pulled on the clean scrubs. It would dry off in time, and she didn't have any choice.

She checked herself in the mirror, then headed back outside and found him propped against the wall of the building on his phone. He glanced at her, nodded and ended the call, slipping the phone back into his pocket.

'Better?'

'I'll do.'

'I really am sorry.'

'As you were kind enough to point out, I ran into you—although technically I wasn't running.'

'Almost, but I wasn't looking where I was going. Why don't we call it quits?' he said with a wry grin, and ushered her into the café. Two minutes later they were sitting outside on a bench and ripping open sandwich packets.

'Coronation chicken or tuna?'

'Don't care. I just want to eat it before my pager goes off.'

He split them, handed her one of each and tore open the potato crisps, and she put their coffee down carefully on the bench between them and bit into the first sandwich.

'So, Annie Brooks, tell me all about yourself,' he said.

She raised an eyebrow at him. 'All?'

He grinned. 'Well, obviously not all. I don't need to know when you started your periods or what grade you got for your A levels—'

'Thirteen, and three As. You?'

He threw back his head and laughed. 'OK. Three As and a B. And I'm still waiting. My mother said it might be a while.'

It was her turn to laugh.

'OK. I'm…single,' she said, reluctant to use the word when it wasn't technically true, because she was definitely in a relationship, albeit with her children. But there didn't seem to be a box to tick for 'was engaged to a philandering adulterer who legged it before I could tell him I was pregnant' so it was hard to find a more appropriate word. And for some reason she didn't want to tell him about all that.

'I trained in London, at King's, and then I worked in various London hospitals, and I'm thirty-six and this is my first consultancy. I work part time, job sharing with Andy, and I work four days a week. Your turn.'

'OK. I'm thirty-two, single, I trained in Nottingham and I've worked in Cambridge and London. My last job was in Great Ormond Street and I'm angling for a consultancy there.'

'Ah. Hence the Paeds.'

'Indeed. And I'm definitely full time. With bells on. So, that's the work thing. How about the rest? Favourite colour, music, film…'

'OK, my favourite colour is green, I'm vegetarian, a member of Greenpeace, my favourite food is—'

'Don't tell me. Peas. Or spinach? Green beans?'

She couldn't suppress the smile. 'You guessed.'

'I sensed a green theme going on and I know for a fact you were lying about being a vegetarian, because you're eating a chicken sandwich.' He smiled ruefully. 'OK. No more prying. Although I wasn't, really.'

She conceded the point and opened up a little. 'Actually, my favourite colour probably is green. Look over there at the new leaves on the trees, that brilliant acid green. Isn't that the most wonderful colour? So full of hope and promise.'

He looked, and with a soft sigh he nodded, his smile somehow sad. 'Yes. Yes, it is,' he said quietly. 'So, if it's not too personal, why are you here, in Yoxburgh?'

'Because my family's here,' she said honestly but without elaboration. 'You?'

'Ditto,' he said, but there was a shadow in his eyes.

There was a question, as yet unformed, poised

on the tip of her tongue when their pagers both beeped.

He pulled his out, glanced at it and stuffed the rest of his sandwich in his mouth as he sprinted for the door, leaving her to deal with the debris of their lunch.

She left their half-finished drinks. She'd had enough coffee-related incidents today without risking another one. It was only when she joined him in Resus and he glanced down at her chest and grinned that she saw the damp imprint of lace on her scrub top. And her nipples, chilly from the light breeze over the damp fabric, had peaked enthusiastically.

She arched a brow primly, covered her top with an apron and pulled on some gloves.

'So, what have we got?' she asked him, all efficiency.

'This is Elizabeth. She slipped and fell over the edge of the kerb. She's got an open tib and fib on the right and query Colles' of the left radius and ulna. She's stable, she's had five of morphine on the way in and I've just given her another five, and she's very coherent, aren't you, Elizabeth?'

'Am I? I don't feel very coherent. That morphine's lovely,' she slurred.

'Good. We're just waiting for X-rays to confirm the fractures. Would you do me a favour, Annie, and check the pulse in that foot? I think it's looking a bit pale.'

'Sure.'

It was. Pale, cold and she didn't like the look of it.

'I've got a pulse, but it's weak.'

He nodded. 'That's what I thought. The orthos are tied up in Theatre. I think it might need a little help before they're free.'

'Elizabeth?'

'Oh, Jerry! Thank goodness you're here.'

'Sorry, darling, I had trouble parking the car.' He grasped her good hand and looked up at them worriedly. 'How is she?'

'Sore, broken, but she'll be all right,' Annie assured him. 'Her leg's a bit of a worry. I think the blood vessels might be pinched, so we want to stretch it out a little and line the bones up better.'

He winced, and squeezed his wife's hand. 'Will you do it under anaesthetic?'

Ed shook his head. 'No need, it's really fast. We'll give her a sedative and she might moan a bit but she won't really know anything about it and she'll come round very quickly. She's had lots of pain relief.'

'Morphine. It's lovely,' she said, smiling up at her husband and looking utterly away with the fairies.

'Oh, dear. You always were a lightweight, my poppet,' he said fondly, and kissed her forehead. 'She just tripped over the kerb and down she went, just like that. I heard the crack from the other side of the car. Horrible.'

'Yes, it's a nasty break, and she'll need surgery to stabilise it. Right, have we got that ketamine drawn up?'

It took moments. Ed took her foot, Annie took her knee and it was done. Her foot went pink and the pulse was instantly better, with only a little moan to show for it.

Jerry looked a bit queasy for a moment, but he hung on, stroking her hair back from her face and kissing her, and as she came round she smiled at him.

'It's all done,' he told her, and she looked surprised.

'Oh. That was quick.'

'That's us,' Ed said with a grin. 'Faster than a speeding bullet. Right, can we have a backslab on that and refer her to the orthopaedic team, please?'

'The wrist fracture's undisplaced,' Annie told him. 'I think we could just put a backslab on that for now, too.'

He nodded. 'OK, Elizabeth, they'll be taking you up to the ward soon to admit you, and then you'll be going to Theatre to fix your leg.'

'Will it be all right?'

'It should be fine, but you might set off the alarms in the airport from now on.'

'Oh, how exciting,' she said with a smile, and Annie chuckled, amazed at her optimism and positivity.

Jerry smiled. 'That's my girl. Always looks on the bright side.'

But his wife frowned. 'Not always. Talking of theatres, we won't be able to go to the play tonight, will we? What a shame. I was so looking forward to it.'

'We'll go another time.' Jerry looked up at them, glancing from Ed to Annie and back. 'I don't suppose either of you two can use these?'

He produced a couple of tickets from his jacket pocket and held them out. 'Tickets for *Arsenic and Old Lace* at the Yoxburgh Playhouse this evening. We're obviously going to be otherwise engaged, and it seems a shame to waste them. And if you can't use them, perhaps you could pass them on?'

'Of course. Thank you, how kind of you. That's very generous.'

'Well, they're no use to us, and there's no point in wasting them. And you've been very kind. All of you have.'

Ed smiled and pocketed the tickets. 'Thank you. We'll make sure they get used. Good luck, Elizabeth. Hope it goes well.'

'I'm sure it will. Thank you for the morphine. I might have to come back for some more of that, it's rather nice.'

He chuckled as Kate wheeled the trolley out,

but she slowed as she passed and murmured something to him.

He just laughed, and then the doors swished shut and he turned to Annie, his eyes thoughtful.

'I don't suppose you're free this evening? I know Kate is, she just told me, but, to be honest I'm not sure I'm brave enough to take her up on it.' There was a smile flickering in the back of his eyes, and she laughed softly.

'She's not that bad.'

'If you say so, but I'd much rather take you.'

She tilted her head on one side and studied him searchingly. 'Are you serious?'

'Of course I'm serious. Why not? We've just been given two free tickets for a very funny play, and frankly I could do with a good laugh and you look as if you could, too. So—are you free to come with me or are you going to make me take Kate?'

Was she free? Free to *go*, yes, if her mother would babysit, and tonight wasn't a night she was usually busy. But—free to *go out* with Dr Gorgeous?

That was an altogether different question and it made her heart beat a little faster.

'I need to check with my family,' she said evasively, and his smile softened.

'Me, too. So, shall we both do that and then confirm?'

'Good idea. I'll let you know.'

'What happened to our coffee, by the way?' he asked as they walked out of Resus together.

'Ah. I left it outside. Thought we'd had enough coffee dramas today.'

His eyes flicked down to her chest, and he smiled, sending all sorts of crazy messages to her nerve endings.

'Probably wise. Want to try again?'

But the red phone and her pager had other ideas, and they headed off in different directions, coffee on hold again.

'Don't forget to let me know,' he called after her, and she nodded.

She still wasn't sure if she wanted to go. No, she was sure that she did, but she wasn't sure—at all—of the wisdom of it. Nevertheless, as soon as she could, she rang her mother.

* * *

'So, are you taking me to the theatre tonight?'

He looked down into Kate's guileless eyes and smiled wryly. 'No. I'm taking Annie, if she's free.'

'Annie?'

'Yes, *Annie*. What's wrong with that?'

Kate shrugged. 'Nothing. Just—she's older than you, and she'll need a babysitter if her mum can't do it.'

Babysitter?

'She's checking it out,' he said smoothly, while his understanding of Annie realigned itself in private. 'And age is nothing to do with it. This is hardly a hot date and, anyway, she's not exactly ancient.'

'Well, if you change your mind, I'm definitely available,' she said, her tempting smile promising to turn it into the hot date of the century.

He wasn't tempted. Not in the least, which was odd because normally he might well have been, but compared to Annie—well, there was no comparison, and he had to put her straight or life was going to be really difficult.

'Thanks, but I'm sure it'll be fine,' he said gently but firmly. 'And for what it's worth, I won't change my mind. Ever. I'm not in the market, Kate, so you're wasting your time with me.'

She smiled ruefully. 'Shame. We could have had fun. Well, if you do change your mind, you know where to find me.'

Did she have no pride?

He went back to work, the word 'babysitter' echoing in his head. Funny. She hadn't mentioned a child. Family, yes, but a child? Not that it changed anything, not for this evening. Or any other evening. He wasn't going there, he reminded himself firmly. Tonight was a definite one-off.

He grabbed the little mid-afternoon lull and went out of the door to call his grandmother.

'Hi, Marnie. How are you doing?'

'OK. What's wrong? You don't usually ring during the day.'

'I wanted to ask you a favour. We've been given tickets to the theatre tonight by a patient. I just wondered if you could cope without me this evening if I went.'

'Of course I can cope. You go and have a lovely time. Are you going with anyone nice?'

He laughed softly. 'I'm going with a colleague. We were both working on the case.'

'Well, have fun with her.'

Her? Damn her razor-sharp intuition. He could challenge her but that would draw attention to it, so he changed the subject. 'How's he been today? Are you sure you can get him to bed all right on your own? Mum and Dad should be around if not.'

'Of course I can do it. As you said, your parents are around if I run into difficulties.'

Although they both knew she wouldn't call them unless there was an out and out crisis. And he could see where they were coming from, how emotionally distressing his father found it, but—

'Are you sure?'

'Of course I'm sure. You go out and have a lovely time, but I expect you to tell me all about it.'

He chuckled. 'OK, will do. I'll see you later. Call if you need me, I'll have my phone on silent but I'll feel it ring and I can always leave. It won't be too late, anyway.'

'I won't need you. You go and have fun. Love you, darling.'

'Love you, too. I'll see you later.'

He hung up and turned round, to find Annie watching him thoughtfully.

'I thought you said you were single?'

He blinked. 'I am. That was my grandmother.'

'Oh.' She coloured slightly and waved a hand. 'Sorry. I'm a bit, um…'

'Suspicious?'

'Sorry,' she said again. 'It's a habit.'

He nodded, then said casually, 'So did you get your babysitter sorted out?'

She stiffened, her eyes widening briefly with alarm, and then she frowned. 'How…?'

'Kate,' he told her, although he didn't tell her what else Kate had said in the process of eliminating the competition.

She rolled her eyes. 'Of course. Silly me.' She gave a wry laugh but she didn't look pleased and so he didn't pursue it. Her dependants were none of his business.

'So—did you sort it?' he asked again, and she nodded.

'Yes. Yes, I did. It's fine.'

'Good. That means we're both free. So, shall I pick you up at seven?'

Panic flared in her luminous blue eyes. 'No. I'll meet you there at a quarter past. It's only a short walk from home and it's a lovely day.'

And you don't want to give me your address.

'OK. I'll be there at seven-fifteen, armed with the tickets. We can have a drink before the show. I'll get them in ready. What would you like?'

'Oh. Um—dry white wine?'

'OK.' He smiled at her, curious that she seemed suddenly flustered by the idea of the drink. 'So—do you want me, or were you just eavesdropping?'

'I want y—' She broke off, and soft colour washed over her cheeks again as she registered what she was saying, but she held his eyes anyway and he suppressed a smile. 'There's a little girl I want you to look at,' she amended.

'OK. Lead me to her, and you can fill me in.'

* * *

This is not a date.

She stared blankly at the contents of her wardrobe, the words echoing in her head like a mantra.

So—what to wear, then? Jeans? Or smart-casual, which opened a whole new can of worms, because there was a huge range of options.

Who was she kidding? Her wardrobe was scanty, to say the least, and apart from work clothes she spent precious little on it because the budget just didn't stretch to pretty stuff she never got to wear.

But there was one thing, a rich sapphire-blue maxi dress in soft jersey that she'd bought last summer that she could dress up or down, and she really, really didn't want to wear jeans and a top *again*. She hardly ever went out. This was the first time in ages, and she *knew* it wasn't a date, but there was no harm in looking nice, was there?

And at least it didn't smell of coffee.

She put it on, ripped it off again and put a strappy white vest top on underneath, then pulled it on again and stood back. Better. Cleavage would send out a whole different message, one she wasn't happy with—and just to be on the safe side, she was wearing a T-shirt bra with moulded cups so her nipples wouldn't show if she got chilly. He'd seen quite enough of them today already.

She slid her feet into some pretty little flat pumps, pulled on a cardi, contemplated and dismissed a necklace and at the last minute spritzed herself with perfume.

It was evening, after all, and she couldn't wear it at work, so why not? She checked her lippy, stood back for another look and then glanced at her watch.

Yikes. She was going to have to run.

'Bye, Mum,' she said, sticking her head round the door.

'Bye, darling. You look lovely. Have a good time.'

'Thanks, I will. Call if you need me, I've got my phone on silent. Got to dash.'

She grabbed her bag, debated a jacket and then went without it. No time to dither, no time to stroll there in a leisurely fashion, just a rapid walk that brought her up the steps to the Yoxburgh Playhouse at a hair past seven-fifteen.

She walked in, went up to the bar and he was standing there waiting for her, looking good enough to eat in a casual linen blazer, jeans and a blinding white shirt open at the neck to reveal that oh-so-masculine throat. He hadn't shaved, and the dark shadow on his jaw just added to the tantalising aura of danger that surrounded him.

His smile made her heart trip faster.

'Hi. Sorry I'm late.'

'You're not—well, only a few seconds. Here, have a drink.'

She took the glass, conscious of the fact that she was windswept, breathing hard and would probably start to glow like a beacon in a moment. 'Thank you.'

'My pleasure. You look lovely, by the way. Pretty dress.'

'Thanks. I don't really have a lot of choice, and it's nice to have a chance to wear it.'

'It suits you. That colour really works with your eyes.'

'What, the shadows underneath?'

He chuckled. 'You really need to learn to take a compliment, Annie.'

Well, no, she didn't. She'd had compliments, bucketloads of them, but they'd all been lies and frankly she didn't care if she never heard another one. As she'd pointed out to him, being suspicious was a habit.

'Sorry. I don't trust compliments.'

He frowned, opened his mouth as if to say something and then shut it again, but his eyes were frank and assessing, and she got the feeling there wasn't much he didn't see.

And that made her uneasy. She didn't want to be the object of his scrutiny, so she changed the subject fast.

'So—remind me of the plot?'

One of those strong, dark eyebrows quirked, but he let her get away with it.

'Oh, it's crazy. Two daffy old sisters who poison their lodgers and bury them in the cellar in graves dug by a brother who thinks he's Teddy Roosevelt and he's digging the Panama Canal, and another brother who's in love with the preacher's daughter. I haven't seen it for years but it's very, very funny.'

'It sounds chaotic. I was trying to remember if I'd ever seen it, but I don't think I have. What a shame about Elizabeth's fall.'

'Mmm. They were really looking forward to it. She's doing OK, by the way. I rang a little while ago and she was out of surgery and back on the ward and it all went well.'

'Good. Well, here's to them.'

She raised her glass, and he clinked his against it and held her eyes with his as he took the first sip.

They smouldered slightly—or was it just her imagination? She looked away, suddenly conscious of his nearness in the now-crowded bar, and she felt the warmth from her brisk walk beginning to make itself felt.

'Gosh, it's getting hot in here,' she said, peeling off her cardi and slinging it over her arm.

'It'll be warm in the auditorium, too. We'd better drink up and go and find our seats.'

'Good idea.' She drained her glass, felt the wine hit her system and wished she'd had a little more to eat before she'd come out. All she needed was to trip over the steps and fall flat on her face.

But she didn't fall, and he held her elbow and ushered her politely to her seat, folding it down for her and then sitting after she was settled.

Bone-deep good manners.

And suddenly she felt safer, less threatened, because for all he was gorgeous, he'd said and done nothing to make her feel uncomfortable. It was just her own reaction to him, and she could manage that. It was under her control.

It would be fine.

And it was, right up until the time the lights dimmed, the audience went quiet and her arm brushed against his in the narrow seats.

He'd taken off his jacket, turned back his sleeves and the soft hairs on his forearm teased her skin, making the tiny hairs on the back of her neck stand to attention.

Heat shot through her, and she shifted subtly, moving slightly out of his way, but there was someone on the other side who was taking the whole armrest, so she shifted back again, right into the warm, fragrant air that surrounded him, the scent of cologne drifting over her and making her want to lean closer and breathe him in.

She resisted the urge, just folded her hands in her lap to keep her elbows out of mischief, and then the action on stage caught her attention and she made herself forget about him and let the experience take over.

'That was so, so funny.'

'Wasn't it? Utterly hilarious. Very physical. I'm surprised some of the cast haven't been in to see us before now. They did Alan Ayckbourn's *Noises Off* when I was in Nottingham, and someone came in with a broken leg from falling down the stairs one too many times.'

'Ouch. The things they do for their art.' Annie tugged her cardi closer round her shoulders as they headed for the street. 'Gosh, it's cooled off. I am an idiot, I nearly brought a jacket but I was running late and it seemed quite warm at seven.'

'Here.'

Before she could protest, she felt the weight of his blazer draped around her shoulders, warm from his body and carrying the scent of his cologne. It was like wearing him, and she breathed in slowly and drew the heady essence of him deep into her lungs.

'Better?'

'Much. Thank you.'

'You're welcome. I could make a wisecrack about you not dressing adequately, but I'm not that mean.'

'No, of course not. Just for that, I won't offer it back.'

'Pride wouldn't let me take it. And anyway, as I've already pointed out, you look lovely so it's a small sacrifice.'

'I'm sure you'll live.'

'I'm sure I will. But it does mean I have to walk you home to repossess it.'

He grinned at her with that little-boy grin, and she smiled back, her eyes softening. 'That's fine, I'll let you. I don't think you're about to turn into a stalker. Thank you for taking me this evening, by the way.'

'You're welcome. Thank you for coming. You

do realise if you hadn't been able to, I would have been obliged to ask Kate.'

She laughed softly at his shudder. 'Why didn't you ask her in the first place? I can't believe you're really scared of her.'

He chuckled. 'No contest. It was you or Kate, and you were the obvious choice. Apart from the fact that Jerry gave us the tickets and not Kate, I'd far rather be with you. I think we have the same sense of humour.'

'And Kate doesn't?'

His mouth quirked. 'Kate isn't interested in humour. She just wants my body.'

Annie spluttered and clapped her hand over her mouth to suppress the laugh. 'That's outrageous!'

'It's true. She as good as said so. I told her I wasn't interested.'

'She'll be gutted. She fell in love with you yesterday when she saw you through the glass.'

He chuckled, but there was a tinge of colour on his neck and it made her smile.

'So—just out of curiosity,' she asked after a moment of companionable silence, 'and feel free to tell me to mind my own business, but who was your grandmother putting to bed?'

'Ah. My grandfather. He's—' Ed broke off, and his face looked troubled.

'Sorry. You don't have to talk about it.'

'That's OK. He's in a wheelchair and he's a bit difficult to deal with sometimes.'

She nodded slowly. 'Is that why you're here? To help with caring for him?'

He looked down at her, surprised by her intuition, but maybe he shouldn't have been because she seemed to be able to read him easily.

'Yes,' he told her, because it was the truth, if not the whole truth. 'He's going downhill fast now, and Marnie really can't manage any longer, but she's determined to look after him herself. I don't know how long he's got, but I promised her I'd be around for her until he's gone.'

'And then?'

He shrugged. 'Who knows?'

'So do you live with them?'

He shook his head, surprising her. 'No. I've got my own place closer to the hospital. I'm renting it from the Walkers. He's an obstetrician. James put me in touch with them when he offered me the job.'

'And does she mind? Your grandmother?'

'No,' he said, but he wasn't sure it was true. 'She would probably rather have had the company, but I told her I needed to be nearer the hospital and she was OK with it.'

'So where do they live?'

'On the clifftop near the golf club.'

She frowned. 'But—that's only about a mile or so away from the hospital.'

'I know, but mine is closer, and that's five minutes in an emergency, and she hasn't questioned it. And I needed my own space.'

'And you couldn't say so.'

He smiled wryly. 'No. Not directly. Not like that.'

Annie nodded slowly. 'Families are tricky things. Juggling all the obligations. The guilt.'

'Tell me about it.' He looked down at her again as they strolled slowly along the pavement. 'So where does your mother live?'

'With me. Or, rather, we live with her. I've got two daughters. Twins. Chloe and Grace.

They're nearly three. She took early retirement and moved down to London to help me when I went back to work, and we lived in my rented flat, but then my grandmother needed more support so we moved back up here to Mum's bungalow when a job came up last summer. I've been here nearly a year and it's been brilliant, but we couldn't afford a big enough house for all of us so we're living in Mum's for now until I've cleared my debts from my maternity leave. It's a bit crowded, though, and sometimes I just long for my own space.'

He nodded. 'I can understand that. Even if it's just for a short while every day, it's important, and I imagine that's even more true with twins. That's pretty hard-core parenting, I should imagine, especially in the early days.' He hesitated for a minute, then went on, 'And their father?'

'Not part of our lives,' she said firmly, and he heard the door slam firmly closed.

That was fine. He had enough no-go areas in his own life to understand she had hers, but it didn't stop him despising a man who could abandon his own children. Some people didn't know how lucky they were.

She'd come to a halt, pausing in front of a small detached bungalow in a leafy avenue just around the corner from his rented house.

'This is me,' she said, and he opened the garden gate and walked her to the door. The porch light wasn't on and the area was shaded from the streetlight by a tree, creating an intimate little space.

Too intimate.

Suddenly the air was filled with tension, crackling with electricity, heavy with expectation and suppressed emotion. His? Hers?

Both?

He couldn't kiss her. It would be crazy. They were colleagues. He'd told his grandmother that. Hell, he'd told Kate that, and he didn't want to muddy the waters at work.

But he wanted to kiss her.

Despite all his best intentions, despite the serious talking-to he'd given himself the night before, he wanted to kiss her.

And she wanted to kiss him. He could feel it,

in the tension coming off her in waves, in the hesitation, the breathless sense of anticipation.

He reached for her, his hands pausing briefly on her shoulders, then common sense intervened and he slipped the jacket off her shoulders and stepped back.

'Goodnight, Annie. I'll see you tomorrow.'

For a nano-second she didn't move, but then he felt the tension snap and she nodded, slipped her key in the lock and vanished inside the door, closing it softly in his face.

He let his breath out on a long, slow sigh, turned on his heel and walked back to the pavement. He hesitated, then turned right instead of left and walked slowly along the quiet streets towards his grandparents' house, deep in thought.

He hadn't kissed her. He'd so nearly done it, but then at the last second he'd bottled out.

No. Not bottled out. Come to his senses, in the nick of time.

The wind picked up, the sea breeze teasing his skin with cool fingers. He shrugged into his jacket, and it was still warm from her body, the scent of her perfume lingering on the fabric, and he realised he hadn't come to his senses at all. He'd just delayed the inevitable.

CHAPTER THREE

ANNIE LEANT AGAINST the front door and blew her breath out slowly.

She'd been *sure* he was going to kiss her, and when he'd moved in like that, reached out for her, she'd *known* he was going to.

And then he'd lifted the jacket off her shoulders.

She'd forgotten about the jacket. Forgotten about all sorts of things, like the fact that *it wasn't a date* and *she wasn't interested in him* and *she didn't do this with anyone, especially not a work colleague!*

She groaned softly and buried her face in her hands, just as her mother came out of the sitting room.

'Annie?'

She lifted her head, brushing her hair back off her face, and smiled. 'Hi. How were the girls?'

'Fine.' Her eyes were searching. 'Are you OK?'

'Yes, of course. I'm just a bit tired all of a sudden.'

'It's not sudden, you're always tired. You have a hectic job. So, how was it? The play?'

'Hilarious. Very, very funny. It's a nice theatre, it's all been done up. You ought to go.'

'I might. I haven't been in there for years. So, did you have ice cream? Someone at book group said it was very good.'

'It was. Really creamy. I had strawberry. It was lovely.'

And Ed had had chocolate, and she'd asked him what it was like and without a word he'd scooped up a dollop and put it in her mouth.

With his spoon.

She'd felt herself melting faster than the ice cream.

'Sorry—what?'

'I said, was it local ice cream?'

Local—? 'Um—I'm not sure. It could have been. Why?'

'Oh, the person at book group said something about that. You can buy it in farm shops round here, apparently, if it's the one she thought. So, did your friend walk you home? I didn't hear a car stop.'

OK. It hadn't taken long, and she'd known it was coming, could almost see the antenna twirling slowly in the background. She nearly laughed at her mother's predictability.

'No, we walked. He was going this way. He lives near here.'

Which might not be a lie, but since he hadn't actually told her where he lived, it was hard to know. But she wasn't telling her mother about borrowing his jacket, or the almost-kiss that wasn't. Using the word *he* was more than enough information.

'Cup of tea?' she asked, heading for the kitchen, and her mother followed her.

'That would be nice. So, was this anyone I know of?'

'The new guy,' she said, busying herself with the mugs and teapot so she didn't have to look her mother in the eye. 'Ed. We were working on the patient together, and they gave us the tickets. It would have been hard to refuse—and, anyway, I never go out. I thought it might be fun. And it was.'

'Well, it was nice of you to go with him. I expect he's a bit lonely if he's new to the area.'

'Oh, he's not, he knows it well. His family all live in the area and I think he was brought up here. That's why he's here—his grandfather's not well. He helps his grandmother with him.'

'Oh, that's kind of him. He was lucky there was a job available.'

'I think we were luckier to get him. He's a great doctor, but he has plans for his future, and they don't involve sleepy old Yoxburgh, so it's definitely temporary,' she said firmly, cutting her mother off at the pass. 'Here, your tea. I think I might take mine to bed and read for a while. My legs are aching, it's been a busy day. Thanks for babysitting for me. You're a star.'

She kissed her mother goodnight and escaped, closing the door of her tiny bedroom with a sigh of relief, but if she imagined she'd shut Ed out, she was wrong.

He followed her in, his laugh, his warm, spontaneous personality, his wicked sense of fun all tormenting her. Wasn't that the first thing always in the personal column adverts? GSOH? Well, he certainly had a good sense of humour, topped off with a lethal dose of masculine charm and looks to die for.

It was a good job he hadn't kissed her. Really. If he'd kissed her, it would have been a disaster. Made it impossible to work together. It was hard enough as it was, and she didn't need to fall into the trap of succumbing to a colleague. Or anyone.

She was rubbish at relationships, rubbish at men in general and good-looking men with smiling bedroom eyes in particular. She needed to remember that.

She plonked down on the edge of the single bed and sighed. She was going to have to get a serious grip on herself before tomorrow.

'So how did it go last night?'

He groaned inwardly. He'd spent the entire night thinking about Annie, and discussing it with Kate was the last thing he needed.

'Fine. Very funny. It was worth going.'

'I meant with Annie. Little Dr Prim, with her sweet little girls and her "don't touch me" attitude.'

He ground his teeth. 'Not that it's any of your business, but we had a good time, thank you.'

'Oh, come on, tell all.'

That was another of the nurses chipping in, grinning and propping her elbows on the high desk, her chin in her hands, her eyes alight with mischief.

'Oh, for heaven's sake, we went to the theatre!' he said, totally exasperated. 'How is this such a big deal?'

'But you went with *Annie*, and Annie doesn't go anywhere with *anyone*.'

So now the receptionist was getting in on the act. Where the hell were the patients when you needed them?

He sighed and rammed a hand through his hair.

'Look,' he said, hanging on to his temper with difficulty, 'we were given two tickets by a patient and her husband, tickets they couldn't use, for a light-hearted slapstick comedy. Annie and I were both there, they offered the tickets to us, we accepted. It would have been churlish not to. And as we were both free, we went. End of.'

'And?'

'And *what*?' he growled.

'Did you kiss her goodnight?'

No, he hadn't, and he'd spent the entire night regretting it. And because he was tired, and tetchy, and because his conscience was still giving him hell for bailing on his grandmother, he lost it.

'No, I did *not* kiss her goodnight!' he snapped. 'I walked her home, I went to my grandparents' house to make sure that my elderly grandmother had managed to get my incredibly frail and terminally ill grandfather into bed on her own, because I'd had the temerity to take a night off and go out and have fun, and then I walked home to my own house and went to bed. Alone. Is that what you wanted to know?'

He glared at them all, one after the other, and they had the grace to look embarrassed. And then he turned on his heel and almost fell over Annie.

And James Slater, the clinical lead.

Great. Marvellous. He shut his eyes.

'Problem?' James asked mildly, and Ed swore softly but pithily under his breath and stalked off. That was the last time he took anyone from work out for any reason at all—

'Ed?'

He stopped walking, and Annie came round in front of him, her eyes troubled.

'They were only teasing. Don't you think you were a little harsh?'

'They were being downright nosy—and they were really bitchy about you. Kate called you Little Dr Prim.'

She flapped her hand dismissively. 'They call me Dr Prim all the time. I don't care.'

'Well, I do, and I care that they think that what either of us chooses to do is in any way their business.'

'You were still nasty to them.'

'Nasty? *Nasty*? I didn't even scratch the surface of *nasty*. I just told them to back off. Hopefully they'll listen.'

'Kate's crying.'

'Kate? Why on earth would she be crying?'

'Because you were really mean? She's not so bad, Ed. She's pretty harmless.'

He rammed a hand through his hair. 'You reckon?'

'I know. They were only teasing you. You should apologise. Bearing in mind you have to work with her.'

He sighed and rammed the hand through his hair again. Actually, he felt like tearing it out, but that wouldn't help anyone. Neither would putting his fist through the wall. His sexual frustration was *certainly* not their business!

'Where is she?' he asked wearily.

'In the sluice.'

He went and found her, standing staring at the wall and sniffing, a wad of tissues in her hand.

'Kate, I'm sorry.'

She glanced at him, then looked away, her eyes welling. 'No, I'm sorry. I never know when to stop. It was only meant to be a joke. I didn't know about your grandfather. I'm so sorry. It must be awful for you all.'

'It is, but that's not your fault, and it's not your

fault you didn't know. I don't talk about him.' He sighed and took a step forward, relenting in the face of her abject apology. 'Come here.'

He pulled her into his arms, hugged her gently and then tipped her head back with a finger. 'Forgive me?'

She nodded, and he gave her a peck on the cheek and let her go.

'I think I can hear the red phone,' he said. 'Don't be long.'

The trauma call came through the speakers at that moment, and he changed direction, heading for Resus.

James was waiting, and he raised an eyebrow. 'Made friends again?'

'Sorry. Yes, we have.'

'Good, because I don't like playground fights in this environment and we all need to be able to work together.'

'We can. It's fine. It won't happen again.'

'Good. Right, let's get to work.'

She found him at lunchtime sitting outside in the sun, staring out across the park and idly shredding a leaf into his lap. He was on their bench—*their* bench?—and she walked hesitantly over to him.

'Mind if I join you?'

He glanced up and shrugged. 'Do I have a choice?'

She froze, wondering where the man she'd laughed with last night had gone, and then she saw the haunted look in his eyes and sat down, ignoring his remark.

'What's up?'

'My grandfather's not good. Marnie was pretty stressed last night. He was a bit feisty.'

'Does he get physical?'

'Only as far as he can, which isn't far. His movement's not great, but it doesn't stop him saying nasty things to her when he gets frustrated.' He sighed and dropped his head back, closing his eyes and shutting everything out.

Or at least that was what it looked like.

'Can she really cope alone?'

'She's not alone. She's got me, and she's got my parents, but they haven't retired yet and my father doesn't get home until seven from his office, and my mother's hardly ever home any earlier, and they're both too tired to be of much use. And anyway, Dad finds watching him deteriorate incredibly stressful and that makes him a bit curt so he always manages to rub my grandfather up the wrong way and then they fall out.'

'And you get on with him?'

He smiled ruefully, but his eyes softened. 'Well, we used to. He was my best friend when I was a kid. My brother and I spent a lot of time there in the school holidays because our parents were both working, and he had endless patience with us. He was a teacher, and he took it seriously and made everything an adventure. We did so many things together, and nothing was too much trouble. He was far more of a father to me than my own father was.'

'So you're balancing the books?'

He nodded slowly. 'Kind of.'

'And where's your brother in all this?'

'London. They live in Dulwich and they have busy lives.'

Which was code for too busy to look after an ailing old man and the wife who was loyally supporting him. Like their parents, who also found it too stressful. And Ed didn't? She wanted to smack them all for leaving him and Marnie to cope alone.

'Have you eaten?'

'No. I'm not hungry.'

'I thought you might say that. I brought you a sandwich.'

She tore it open and pulled out one of the halves and put it in his hand. 'It's a BLT.'

'Thanks.' He bit into it absently, and while he had his mouth busy, she sucked in a breath and said what was on her mind.

'About last night.'

He coughed, choking on the sandwich, and she handed him her coffee.

'What about last night?' he asked when he could speak.

'I just wanted to say thanks again for taking me, and don't worry, I didn't get any ideas because of it.'

He met her eyes, the sandwich forgotten, and his mouth tipped into a wry, self-deprecating smile. 'That's a shame, because I had ideas all night. Not that I intend to act on them. The last thing I've got time for in my life at the moment is a relationship, and I know you're not that kind of girl.'

'What kind of girl?'

His smile faded. 'The kind who doesn't expect anything except a good time. One who knows the rules.'

'Oh, I know the rules,' she said bitterly. 'Don't let anyone close. Don't believe a word they tell you. Especially don't believe it when they ask you to marry them, because the chances are they aren't free and they're just doing it because they know if they don't, you'll walk because it's going nowhere, but it's going nowhere anyway because he's a lying bastard and he has a wife and kids and a whole other life back home in the States—'

She clamped her lips shut, and after a stunned silence she heard him let out his breath slowly.

'Ouch.'

'Yes. Ouch. Sorry, I didn't mean to say all that.'

'Don't worry about it. Is that why he's out of your life?'

She laughed shortly. 'That and the fact that he's gone home to wifey to try and sort out the train wreck that's his marriage.'

'Does he even know about the girls?'

She shook her head, and Ed felt a wave of shock.

'Wow.'

'It's fine. My mother brought me up on her own after my father died, and if she can do it, so can I.'

'So do they have a father figure?'

'No—not nearby. My grandfather died three years ago, just weeks before they were born, and I'm an only child. There's just me, my mother and my grandmother. And Chloe and Grace.'

'Four generations of women. Wow.'

'We manage. I make sure I don't tell them that men are poisonous.'

'We aren't all poisonous,' he corrected softly, and she turned her head and met his eyes and smiled.

'I know. My father wasn't, and my grandfather wasn't, and I've got uncles and cousins so it's not quite as bad as all that.' She tipped her head on one side, studying him thoughtfully. 'I'm sure Kate would know the rules.'

He frowned. 'Why do you keep throwing Kate at me?'

She shrugged. 'Because I think you're lonely? Because I think you need someone to share the burden with, someone to take your mind off what's happening? Someone to have fun with?'

'So why Kate? If you know the rules, why not you?'

She stared at him for a second, shocked, and then gave a strangled laugh and looked away hastily. 'Me?' she squeaked, and her heart thudded.

'Why not?' he asked, slightly shocked himself that he'd suggested it, but the idea was growing on him by the second. 'We get on, neither of us wants a permanent relationship, we both have our reasons for that even though they're very different, but it means there won't be any misunderstandings, any broken hearts and tears and threats and disappointment. Just—fun.'

Fun? She stared down at her hands. They were knotted together, the knuckles white, and she was sure he could feel the tension radiating off her. It was so long since she'd had fun she'd forgotten all about it. 'So, let me get this right, you're suggesting—what? A no-strings affair? Casual sex?'

'No.'

His voice was curiously intense, and she looked up and met his eyes. 'Nothing casual about it, but you don't want relationship hassles, I don't want anyone expecting wedding bells, so why not? Not casual, but carefully tailored to fulfil our needs without crossing those boundaries. And more than sex. Much more. I'd like to think we could be friends as well.'

Her heart thudded again. 'Friends with benefits?'

His mouth quirked into a wry smile. 'If you like.'

Did she? It was a crazy idea, but she was so tempted. Ludicrously tempted. A shiver of something dangerously exciting ran through her, and she looked away in case her eyes were too revealing.

'Can I think about it?' she asked, after an age, and she heard his breath ease out on a sigh.

'Of course you can. Take as long as you like. There's no pressure, Annie. And I'll fully understand if it's no.'

She nodded, and got to her feet.

'I'll let you know.'

Good grief. She couldn't believe she was even thinking about it, giving it serious consideration, but she was, all through her shift, and on the following day while he wasn't at work, and then she was off herself and he was back on again, so it was Monday before she saw him. And she'd had plenty of time to think.

Too much.

Time to think herself into all sorts of hot water. But not, apparently, enough time to think herself back out of it again, because she walked into the department on Monday morning, took one look at him and knew what her answer was going to be.

He met her eyes over the central workstation

and after a second his mouth flickered into a smile. 'Hi.'

'Hi. How was your weekend?'

'Chaos, thank you. How was yours?'

'Lovely. We played on the beach, and did a bit of gardening, and went to the playground. And we had a picnic and I caught the sun.'

'I can see.' She had a touch of pink across her nose and cheekbones, and a smattering of tiny freckles was starting to appear. God, he wanted to kiss her. He must have been nuts to walk away.

'So, what have we got?'

'A dislocated patella, a fractured femur, an acute abdomen, query minor head injury—'

'Give me the abdomen. You can have the femur.'

'I was about to tackle the patella. The orthos are coming down to the femur.'

'When did you last check him?'

'Her—and ten minutes ago, but could you do it, before you do the abdo? I want to get the patella back in now and put him out of his misery.'

'So why not get the orthos to do it while they're here?'

'Because he's already had the ketamine, and anyway I like patellas.'

And with a cheeky wink he picked up the notes and walked off, whistling softly, and left her looking after him and trying not to give herself away too hopelessly.

'He is *so-o-o* cute.'

'Kate, get over it,' she said firmly, trying not to think how cute he was and what she was going to do with him. 'Want to help me with the abdo?'

'Sure.' Kate pushed herself away from the desk and followed her, and nothing more was said about him, to Annie's relief.

Not that it stopped her thinking…

'Can I ask you something?'

'Sure. Does this need a coffee?'

'Maybe.' She chewed her lip. She still hadn't quite committed herself to this crazy idea, but she was tempted. Oh, so tempted. 'Have you got time?'

'I have at the moment. The patella's being put

in a cast, the femur's gone off to Theatre, and the head injury is under observation. How's your abdomen?'

She sucked it in automatically at the mention of the word. '*My* abdomen?' she said, arching a brow at him.

He glanced down and grinned. 'Well—not yours. Yours is obviously fine.'

'Only fine?' she asked provocatively, and then could have kicked herself for flirting with him. 'Whatever. My abdo,' she said hastily, grabbing the conversation and steering it rapidly on to the right track again, 'is under obs. I'm not sure what it is. Not appendix, I don't think, but I'm not sure. There's a fairly convoluted history. I'm waiting for the GP to call me back on my mobile.'

He nodded. 'Abdomens are funny things. There's a whole world of stuff in there. Kids with acute abdomens are a nightmare. Two cappuccinos, please. Take out.'

He handed over the money, gave her her coffee and steered her out of the door. 'I take it this is a private conversation?'

She felt herself colour. 'I just wanted to clarify things.'

'OK.' He sat down, patted the bench beside him and shifted so he was looking at her. 'Clarify what?'

She looked away. Those dark, grey-blue eyes with the navy rims were disconcerting, and this was hard enough.

'This...relationship,' she said, for want of a better word. 'Are we talking exclusivity?'

He let out a short huff that could have been laughter. He sounded slightly stunned.

'Of course! What did you think—I was going to run a string of women? I hardly have time to sleep as it is. No.' He reached out a hand, turned her face gently towards him and shook his head slowly. 'No way is there anyone else even on my radar at the moment. My life is already hellish complicated, Annie. I need time out—from work, from my grandfather, from...'

From the ramifications of his potential inheritance. 'From all sorts of things,' he finished.

She watched him, saw the sadness flicker in

his eyes again, the desperation. 'So, let me get this right. You're looking for—respite care?'

He laughed softly, his eyes crinkling. 'Pretty much. I'd rather call it me time.'

'Me time? I could use some of that.'

'Was that a yes?'

'I don't know,' she said honestly, but her heart was pounding. 'I don't know how we'd arrange it.'

'You could come to me. My house is just round the corner from yours, a three-minute walk. You can come in the back way, it's more anonymous. And it's utterly private. I don't know my neighbours, and I don't have time to get to know them. Nobody will know who you are.'

'But when?'

'Whenever we're both free. Whenever your mother is able to let you go.'

She chewed her lip. Oh, Lord. Her mother. 'I'll have to tell her,' she said, and closed her eyes.

'Is that a problem?'

'Only that she'll know what we're doing.'

'You could tell her you're playing bridge.'

'Late at night? More likely poker.'

He laughed again, and she felt the huff of his warm breath against her skin. 'Annie, don't sweat it. Tell her you're going to the cinema, going for a walk—anything.'

'Lie?'

'No! Just—keep it private. Between us.'

'Private sounds good,' she said quietly. 'I don't want anyone knowing. They just ask questions, and I don't need that.'

'Nor do I. Don't worry, I won't tell anyone. Especially not anyone here. The rumour mill is rife as it is just because we went to the theatre. Oh, which reminds me, I sent some flowers to Elizabeth as a thank-you for the tickets, and Jerry popped in this morning to thank me. She's doing well.'

'Good. And talking of telling each other things, I think you should know Kate thinks you're cute, by the way.'

'Cute? *Cute*?'

He sounded disgusted, and she laughed at him. 'What's wrong with cute?'

'Little girls are cute,' he said, his disgust evident, and she suppressed her laughter, but then his expression changed, his eyes searching hers. ‘So—is that a yes?’

Trapped by those amazing, expressive eyes, she stared up at him and her heart thumped against her ribs.

‘Yes,’ she said slowly. ‘That’s a yes.’

CHAPTER FOUR

THE REST OF the day crawled by.

She admitted her acute abdo, moved on to a wrist fracture, dealt with indigestion that turned out to be a partially blocked coronary artery and went home, her emotions in turmoil.

She was meeting him that evening at his house, at nine. Time for her to put the girls to bed and get ready, time for him to finish his shift and put his grandfather to bed and come home. She'd phoned and asked her mother already if she would mind babysitting that evening, made the excuse of being busy at work to avoid getting trapped into a difficult conversation, and now she was walking up the path to the matriarchal version of the Spanish Inquisition.

Not that her mother would ask any questions, or anything. She didn't need to. She'd just look, and *know*, in that uncanny way mothers had.

Annie understood that. She was beginning to do it herself. Which made it even more disturbing.

The girls, however, were on their own, to her relief, kneeling up at the dining table in a riot of paper and crayons.

'Mummy!'

The welcome, as ever, centred her and she crossed over to them, bathed in the sunshine of their smiles.

'Hello, my lovelies,' she said, hugging them and admiring their drawings, and then her mother came back into the room and her guilt came rushing back to haunt her.

'Hello, darling. Good day?' she asked, putting the kettle on, and then without missing a beat asked, 'What time are you going out?'

'Just before nine,' she said, and she could feel colour crawling up her neck and heading for her face. 'I'll just go and change out of my work clothes.'

She fled, shutting herself in her room and pressing herself against the inside of the door. She could feel her heartbeat, a steady, insistent throb that echoed throughout her body, and she did *not* want to have this conversation with her mother in front of the children!

Should she lie?

Maybe, this time at least, because if it was a total disaster, if he took one look at her naked body and wanted to run, then she wouldn't have the humiliation of having to explain to her mother why it wouldn't be happening again.

Cutting off that line of thought before she talked herself out of going, she stripped off her clothes, pulled on her jeans and a T-shirt and went back to the kitchen and normality. 'That's better. Oh, is that tea for me? Thanks, Mum.'

She sat down at the table with the children and listened to their chatter with half an ear. There had been a bit of a ruckus at nursery. One of the boys had pushed one of the girls over, and he'd been made to stand on the naughty spot *all day*! Well, according to Chloe it had been all day, but Grace thought it was only after milk and biscuits, so that wasn't all day. All day was breakfast to supper, wasn't it?

'I expect it felt like all day,' she said, mediating with the bit of her brain that wasn't wondering what on earth she'd agreed to. 'Right, girls, put the crayons away, please, it's nearly time for your bath and bed.'

'But I haven't finished!' Chloe protested.

'So put it away and finish it tomorrow. Come on, it's bathtime and if you mess around now you won't get a story.'

Chloe put it away. Stories were sacrosanct, and the mere suggestion was enough to ensure her cooperation. If it hadn't been, Grace would have taken the picture from her and put it away herself, she thought with an inward smile.

She chivvied them into the bathroom, perched on the loo and listened to more of the little boy's misdemeanours as the girls played in the bath and soaped themselves.

'Don't get your hair wet, it doesn't need washing tonight,' she reminded them, and then one by one she dried them, cleaned their teeth and sent them to get into their pyjamas.

They had two stories, mostly because she felt so guilty about the 'me time' that was coming that she was overcompensating, and then, unable to stall any longer, she tucked them up in bed and went to brave her mother.

'Gosh, that smells good,' she said, going back into the kitchen.

'Shepherd's pie. Nice and simple, and the girls love it.'

'I love it, too. I can't tell you how much I appreciate coming home every evening to a cooked meal and safe, happy children. Will you marry me?'

Her mother laughed and hugged her. 'Silly girl. I'd be lonely without you all.'

'Well, good, because it's not likely to happen.'

And seamlessly, as if the two thoughts were connected, which they probably were, knowing her mother, she said, 'So, where are you going tonight? Anywhere nice?'

Her heart skipped a beat. 'I'm meeting Ed for a drink,' she told her. It was the truth, or as close to it as she intended to get. She was sure that at some point in the proceedings they'd have a drink, and it was a nice simple social thing that didn't necessarily have any massive implications.

Except that of course it did, for them, and she felt her heart thump and the colour creeping up again towards her cheeks.

'That's nice,' her mother said, setting the pie dish on the table and pulling up her chair. 'So what are you going to wear?'

'Oh, nothing smart,' she said, wondering herself what would be appropriate. Lacy underwear? *No underwear*—?

'Jeans and a top?' she offered hastily, mentally fanning herself.

'Will you be inside or out? It can get chilly if you're sitting outside at the pub.'

'Oh, I doubt if we'll do that. It's a bit breezy today.' *Especially with no underwear*—

'Well, take a jacket just in case. There's nothing worse than being too cold.'

Cold? *Cold*? Not a chance she'd be too cold. She was practically catching fire at the thought of what was to come. The only thing that was stopping her from spontaneous combustion was the little icy finger of dread crawling up her spine at the thought of taking off her clothes in front of someone so beautiful and having to endure the disappointment in his eyes.

'I'll take a jacket,' she said. 'I'm going to walk there and back in any case. Yum, this is delicious. Thank you. So, what have you been up to today? Done anything nice?'

So there it was.

Number fifty-six, in shiny letters on the gate. She glanced up and down the street, but it was deserted, and she opened the gate and went through into the carport. There was a car in there, a sleek, wicked-looking BMW convertible that had *bad boy* written all over it, and as she closed the gate she heard the scrape of a chair and he ducked through a curtain of wisteria and walked slowly towards her.

He was dressed, like her, in jeans, with a washed-out blue cotton shirt open at the neck, and he looked good enough to eat. He gave a slight smile, and she thought he looked—relieved?

He stopped a few feet away. 'Hi. I wasn't sure

you'd come,' he admitted, and the touch of vulnerability took away some of her nerves.

'I said I would,' she told him, although she'd hesitated at the gate. Her heart was trying to climb out of her chest, her mouth was dry and her legs felt like boiled noodles, but he held out his hand and she walked up to him and put her hand in his, and he drew her to his side, dropped a gentle, undemanding kiss on her cheek and ushered her through the trailing wisteria to the secluded garden.

It was beautiful, heavy with the scent of honeysuckle, touched with the last rays of the evening sun, and it enclosed them in a little green haven. It could have been the garden of Eden, and any minute now she expected the serpent to appear with an apple.

No serpent. Just Ed, his hand warm on her spine, leading her to a little bistro set tucked into a sheltered corner. 'I've got a bottle of Prosecco on ice, or if you don't fancy that I have wine, juice, tea and coffee—all sorts,' he said.

There was an ice bucket on the table, next to a pair of elegant champagne flutes and a cluster of bowls, and she sat down just before her legs gave way.

'Prosecco sounds lovely. Thank you.'

'You're welcome. How was your mother about it?'

'Fine. I told her I was going for a drink with you.'

'Well, you're not lying, then, are you?' he murmured, and twisted the cork out with a soft pop. Vapour poured like smoke out of the open neck of the bottle, and he poured the wine carefully into the glasses, put the bottle back on ice and then handed her a glass.

'To us,' he said softly, and she met his smouldering eyes and felt the heat in them spread through her body like wildfire.

'To us,' she repeated, and then she didn't quite know what to say, so she dragged her eyes away from his before she drowned in their midnight depths.

He snagged a handful of nuts and sat down, sprawling back in the chair and crunching them up with those almost perfect, even teeth, and she reached for an olive and bit into it for something to do.

The tension was palpable, and she took a sip of the Prosecco. Bubbles tickled her nose and she wrinkled it, and he smiled. 'Tickles, doesn't it?' he murmured, and she nodded.

His eyes searched hers, and he smiled ruefully. 'Annie, relax. We're having a drink. That's all.'

That was all? She felt the tension drain out of her like a punctured balloon, and then a wash of something that felt curiously like disappointment.

'OK.'

He chuckled and leant forward. 'It doesn't have to be all,' he clarified. 'It could be more.' And his eyes trapped hers and dragged her in.

More? Oh, Lord, she wanted more...

'Why don't we start with the drink?' she said, almost managing to keep the squeak out of her voice, and his mouth kicked up at the side.

'Good idea. How are the kids?'

'Fine,' she said, not wanting to think about the fact that she was a mother. Not now, not in this situation. It seemed—inappropriate, somehow, as if that was another person. 'How's your grandfather?'

'Rubbish.' His smile died, and he looked away. 'He's going downhill. I don't know how long he's got, but I hope it's not much longer. It's just so painful to watch, and it's tearing my grandmother apart.'

'I'm sorry.'

'Yeah.' He was silent for a moment, then he took a breath and turned back to her. 'I meant to tell you, there's a little wooden playhouse in their garden. They had it for my brother's children, but they've outgrown it. I wasn't sure if you'd got room for it or if you'd want it, but you're welcome to it if it's any use.'

'Oh, Ed, thank you. The girls would love a playhouse! Does it come to pieces?'

'I'm sure it will. I'm not sure how. It might be bolted together. I'll have a look. It needs new felt on the roof, but otherwise it's fine.'

'Don't they mind?'

He smiled sadly. 'Grumps is past caring and Marnie would love it to go to a good home. I was talking about you yesterday, and she mentioned it.'

That surprised her. 'You were talking about me?'

'Well—yeah. She has a way of getting things out of me,' he admitted ruefully.

Annie gave a hollow laugh. 'Sounds like my mother. We'll have to make sure they never meet. We wouldn't have a secret left.'

He chuckled and topped up her glass. She hadn't even realised it was empty. She was obviously drinking faster than she'd realised. Nerves? Probably. She was terrified this was going to be a disaster, terrified he'd take one look at her and run, terrified he'd break her heart if she gave him the chance. What was she *doing*? She grabbed a couple of olive breadsticks to blot up the alcohol. 'These are really nice.'

'They are.' He took one, too, then reached for another one at the same time as her and their fingers brushed. Heat shot up her arm like lightning, and she gave a little involuntary gasp and pulled her hand back.

Their eyes clashed—and held.

Her heart started to race, her lips parted, her mouth dried. She swallowed, and slid the tip of her tongue over her dry lips, and he sucked in a breath. Audibly.

For what seemed like minutes but was probably only a few seconds, they sat there, eyes locked, unmoving, and then he got slowly, deliberately, to his feet.

Without breaking the silence he put the breadstick down with exaggerated care and held out his hand to her. Her breadstick fell to the floor, unheeded, and she took his hand and let him pull her up. Gently, inch by inch, he eased her up against him, bent his head and touched his lips to hers, and her body went up in flames.

'Ed…'

She breathed his name against his lips, and he lifted his head, staring down into her eyes as if looking for an answer, and clearly he found it.

'Not here,' he growled softly, and, threading his fingers through hers, he towed her in through the conservatory, through the open kitchen dining space, up the stairs and into the front bedroom.

It was white.

Pure white. All of it, the whole house.

Like a sanctuary, she thought, cool and calm and safe.

And then he cupped her face in his strong, long-fingered hands, bent his head and kissed her, and her brain emptied of everything except sensation.

His mouth was hot.

Hot, firm, his lips slightly damp so they clung to hers, tugging them as he nipped and suckled. She felt his tongue stroke the crease between her lips, and her mouth opened, parting for him, his tongue following, delving, probing.

She delved back, duelling with him, dragging a groan up from deep inside his chest.

She felt her legs buckle, but he grabbed her, hauling her hard up against him so she felt the heat pouring off him, the pressure of his erection, the pounding of his heart against her breasts.

And the need. Oh, God, the need. She felt it too, felt the wanting, the desperation, the compulsion to tear off their clothes and feel his skin against hers.

She pushed him away, and he dropped his hands, stepped sharply back and met her eyes. He was fighting for control, struggling for breath, and his eyes were wild.

'Do you want me to stop?' he asked, his voice ragged, and she gave a fractured laugh, her nerves driven out by something far greater.

'Only if you want me to kill you.'

His eyes shut briefly, and when he opened them she was smiling. 'Hell's teeth, Annie. Come here, woman.'

He pulled her back gently into his reach, his fingers shaking as he undid her blouse one infuriating little pearly button at a time. Why the hell hadn't she worn the jersey dress? One move and it would have been off, and he'd be touching her, holding her, burying himself inside her—

Hanging on to his control by a thread, he peeled the blouse back over her shoulders, trapping her arms, and then he let his eyes rake her breasts.

Pretty, delicate lace encased them, coffee and

cream. He wondered idly if it was the same bra he'd soaked in coffee the other day. Hell, if he'd only known this was underneath those scrubs…

He swore under his breath, lowered his head and trailed his tongue slowly, so slowly around the edge of the lace, blowing lightly over the damp skin. She whimpered, but he didn't stop. Instead he slid one hand up her back, fisted it in her hair and pulled her head back gently, his mouth trailing upwards, over her throat, pausing in the hollow where her pulse was pounding.

He could feel it under his tongue, the heavy throb of her need. Good. He wanted her with him every step of the way.

She whimpered again, writhing against him. 'Kiss me…'

'I am.'

Not like that. More…

His lips moved along her jaw, up to her ear, his tongue brushing the lobe and sending arrows stabbing through her core.

'Ed, *please…*'

He lifted his head and stared down at her. 'Tell me what you want.'

Oh, mercy.

'You,' she said bluntly. 'Right now. I've been thinking about this for days and— Oh!'

She landed in the middle of the bed, arms still trapped behind her by her sleeves, and he unzipped her jeans.

'Lift up,' he ordered, and she dug her heels in, lifted her bottom and he stripped the jeans off her legs and threw them on the floor. One finger hooked into the top of her tiny lace shorts, and he gave a little tug. She lifted again, and he eased them down, down, over her knees, past her calves, over her ankles, his eyes following them every inch of the way.

They fell to the floor, and she lay there staring up at him, propped on her elbows and feeling desperately vulnerable, while his eyes raked her body dispassionately.

No. That was wrong. He looked up at last, and there was nothing dispassionate about the fire that burned in those eyes. He wanted her as badly as she wanted him, and she squirmed with frustration.

'Please…'

The word came out jagged and broken, and his mouth kicked up in a teasing, wicked smile. 'Since you ask so nicely.'

He didn't hang about. He pulled his shirt off over his head, shucked his jeans and boxers in one movement, and then reached for a foil packet.

'Let me.'

She struggled up, freeing her arms at last from the wretched blouse, and took it from him, rolling the condom slowly, firmly down the silken shaft of his erection.

He sucked in his breath, held it for a second then tipped her backwards, coming down on top of her, every muscle taut with control. Her legs wrapped around him, drawing him closer as he surged into her, filling her and bringing tears of relief to her eyes, and she clung to his shoulders, her fingers digging in, gripping him as he drove into her again.

'Oh, that's so good,' he ground out, and then he rolled over, taking her with him, lying flat on his back as he looked up at her.

'And that's even better,' he murmured, his

hands reaching up and cupping her breasts, still in the confines of her bra. 'Take it off for me. I want to see you.'

She hesitated for a second, swamped by doubts again. Her breasts were no longer pert and firm. She'd fed twins, for heaven's sake! But he arched a brow in mock impatience, so she sucked in a breath and reached behind her back, arching a little to do it, and he lifted his hips and she gasped. 'Ed—'

'Nice?'

'*Nice* isn't really the word,' she gritted, and he gave a slow, warm laugh that vibrated deep inside her.

The bra dropped away, freeing her breasts, and for a moment she held her breath. She needn't have worried. He lifted his hands, cradled them gently and sighed.

'Oh, that's better,' he murmured, his thumbs grazing gently over her nipples, dragging out every last ounce of sensation until she cried out and writhed against him. And then he smiled that wicked smile again and started moving, and she felt the tension grip her tighter, felt it spiral up until at last he flipped her beneath him, pinning her down as he drove into her again and again and took her with him over the edge into freefall.

Wow.

Just—wow.

He hadn't really expected this. He'd been half joking when he'd asked her. Not that he hadn't meant it, but he'd never for a moment imagined she'd take him seriously, far less say yes.

And she'd blown him away, with her openness, her courage, her astonishing responsiveness. He still couldn't quite believe it had happened.

He touched her face gently with his fingertips, and she tilted her head towards him and smiled shyly. 'Hi.'

'Hi, yourself. OK?'

Her smile widened, and she nodded. 'Very OK.'

'Good. I'll be back in a moment,' he murmured. He eased his arm out from under her, snagged his jeans off the floor and headed for the bathroom, then went downstairs, locked the back gate, brought the Prosecco and nibbles back in on the tray and carried them up to the bedroom.

'Interval refreshments,' he said with a wicked grin, and got back into bed beside her, propping himself up against the pillows and holding out her glass.

She sat up cross-legged in the bed, tucked the quilt around her and took the glass from him. 'Thanks. I wondered where you'd gone.'

His grin was wry. 'I thought a little security might be in order. We left the back gate unlocked and the doors hanging open.'

'Ah.'

'And the Prosecco downstairs.'

'Bad move. That would have been a waste.' She sipped, then frowned, and he could see reality starting to intrude. 'What time is it? I forgot to put my watch on after my shower.'

'Ten past ten.'

Her shoulders dropped. 'Oh. That's good. I thought it must be later.'

'What time is your mother expecting you home?'

She shrugged, lifting her shoulders and causing the quilt to slip enticingly. 'I told her it would probably be elevenish.'

His smile was slow and lazy, and full of promise.

'Good,' he murmured. 'That gives us lots more time. Drink up.'

He walked her home.

'You don't need to,' she told him, but he just arched a brow.

'Yes, I do,' he said, his voice implacable, and he walked her right to the door.

She turned to him, unsure what to say. *Thank you for the best sex of my life?* That didn't seem quite appropriate, but it was the truth.

In the end she just looked up at him, and he smiled knowingly. 'We should do that again some time,' he said innocently, and she nearly laughed out loud.

'That would be lovely.'

She went up on tiptoe and pressed a fleeting kiss to his cheek. 'Thank you.'

'My pleasure.'

This time there was no mistaking the meaning in his eyes, and she swallowed and took a step back. 'Goodnight.'

'Goodnight, Annie. Sweet dreams.'

He didn't kiss her goodnight. He'd already done that very thoroughly before they'd left the house, but he stayed there until she was safely inside.

She closed the door quietly and leant against it, centring herself, listening to the sound of his retreating footsteps. The television was still on in the sitting room, and she went in, wondering if she looked as thoroughly loved as she had been, and smiled brightly at her mother.

'Hi. Want a cup of tea?'

'No, thanks, darling. I'm just watching the last five minutes of this and I'm off to bed. Good time?'

'Yes, thanks. Very nice.'

Hardly the word, but there you go. But it had been nice in many ways. Very nice. Nice to have time to herself, nice to be the focus of someone's undivided attention, nice to be so thoroughly and spectacularly loved.

Except it wasn't love, and she didn't want it to be. And neither did he.

But it had certainly been spectacular.

Win-win.

'I think I'll just get a glass of water and go to bed, then, if you're not staying up,' she said, glad she didn't have to stay and chat while her mother grilled her. 'Thanks for looking after the girls. I take it they didn't wake up?'

'No, they're fast asleep, I haven't had a peep out of them.'

'Bless you. I'll go and tuck them up. 'Night, Mum.' She dropped a kiss on her mother's cheek, checked the girls and went into the bathroom. She caught a glimpse of her naked body in the mirror, and her eyes widened.

Whisker-burn, over her nipples, around her collar bone, a touch of it across her lip.

She touched it, remembering the feel of his mouth, the slight rasp of stubble on her body. So, so sexy. And he hadn't recoiled in horror when he'd seen her. Far from it. He'd even come back for more…

Smiling to herself, she cleaned her teeth, took off her make-up and went to bed.

* * *

He strolled slowly home, the smile that wouldn't seem to fade teasing the corners of his mouth.

For some crazy reason, probably because it had been a while, he'd been really wound up before she'd arrived, but her own nerves had calmed him and once he'd kissed her, any hesitation had gone. Well and truly.

He blew his breath out slowly through his mouth. She'd been so responsive, so warm, so ready, so generous. She'd held nothing back, and neither had he, and it had been amazing.

As far as he was concerned, the evening had been a definite success. He was pretty sure she agreed, but time would tell. He'd see her at work in the morning. Sheesh. That would be a challenge. It had been difficult enough before.

He shut the gate behind him and locked it, then walked across the garden. There was a crunch, and he looked down and saw the breadstick on the paving. She'd dropped it when he'd pulled her to her feet, right before he'd kissed her. He closed his eyes briefly as the memory crashed over him, leaving fire in its wake.

He wanted her again. Now. This minute.

But he couldn't have her. There was a time and a place, and this wasn't it.

He sent her a text.

Great evening. Thank you. See you tomorrow.

His phone pinged, and he pulled up the reply.

The pleasure was all mine ;-) A x

He smiled, keyed in his reply and hit Send.

Two streets away, Annie opened his reply.

I think not. We should check it out again some time soon.

She grinned. It couldn't be soon enough.

Whenever you're ready.

She typed with her lip caught between her teeth, excitement and anticipation fizzing in her veins.

She hit Send, put the phone down on her bedside table, snuggled down under the quilt and lay there hugging her feelings to her chest. He'd been—amazing, really. Warm, funny, sexy—oh, yes, so-o-o sexy—and after the initial few moments he'd seemed more relaxed than she'd ever seen him.

She thought about his grandfather, and ached for him. He was gutted. It was obvious how much he loved the old man, obvious how much they were all hurting. No wonder he'd needed this so much, a time out from the inescapable reality of life and death.

Old age could bring many joys and pleasures, but it could also bring great sadness. She knew this. She'd lost her father before she was old enough to understand, but she'd watched her grandmother and mother cope with the loss of her own grandfather only a few years ago, and she knew first-hand the impact such a loss had on a family.

Well, that was fine. He could chill out with her, take time out from the hellish emotional roller coaster they were riding, and she could have some simple, uncomplicated fun, something that had been sorely lacking from her life for the past three years.

Except for the girls. The girls were fun, great fun, and she adored them, but tonight…

Tonight had been personal.

Deeply personal, she thought, and heat washed through her again at some of the things he'd done to her. She was sure they'd barely scratched the surface of his repertoire, but it hadn't for a moment felt sordid or tacky. Far from it. He'd made her feel special, cherished. Beautiful.

She rolled to her side, hugged her pillow close and waited for sleep to come. She wouldn't sleep, she knew that. She was so wired—

The yawn caught her by surprise. Her muscles ached, she felt tired and relaxed, as if she'd just had a workout. Her mouth tilted into a sleepy smile. Funny, that…

CHAPTER FIVE

THE FOLLOWING DAY was—well, to call it interesting was an understatement.

Every time he turned round, Annie was there, and now that he knew exactly what was under her scrubs, he was finding it increasingly difficult to keep his body under control.

She bent over to get something out of a cupboard, and he groaned. Scratch difficult. He was finding it impossible. Utterly impossible.

He found himself some admin to do, sitting at a desk with his back to her, but he knew she was there, his radar now so attuned to her that he could sense her distance from him down to microns.

'Paediatric trauma call, five minutes. Paediatric trauma call, five minutes.'

Thank God.

He shot the chair back and headed for Resus.

* * *

'Have you and Ed fallen out?'

Annie flicked a quick glance at Kate and looked away again hastily. 'No, of course not.' *Far from it.*

'Are you sure? Because for two people who are supposedly speaking, you're both doing a fine job of ignoring each other.'

'Rubbish. What makes you say that?'

Kate rolled her eyes and sighed. 'Annie, you haven't so much as *looked* at him today if you haven't had to! And he hasn't looked at you either—well, not openly. There's been the odd sly glance—'

Annie snapped the file shut and turned to Kate. 'There have been no *sly* glances, we aren't *not speaking*, we're just busy and we haven't had occasion to. Mrs Grover's results are back, she's fine. Please discharge her and tell her to go to her GP if she gets a recurrence of her symptoms.'

She thrust the notes at Kate and headed for Resus, determined to prove her wrong, and looked Ed straight in the eye.

'Need any help with this one?'

He looked straight back, utterly professional, focused on the job. Wow, he was good. If she hadn't seen him lose control so spectacularly in her arms yesterday, she wouldn't have believed it.

'Could do. Seven-year-old boy, fallen onto his arm from a climbing frame in a school playground. Sounds like a very nasty fracture. I've contacted the ortho team but we need to assess him for head and other injuries. Possible LOC briefly at the scene, they aren't sure.'

She nodded. 'OK. Are you leading?'

'If that's all right?'

She nodded again. 'Sure. You're the paeds guru.'

Their patient arrived a moment later, a skinny, gangly boy with a chalk-white face and a mother who didn't look much better. The paramedic filled them in.

'This is Oliver Wells. He missed a handhold on the climbing frame and fell six feet onto a rubber mat, but he landed awkwardly on his left arm.'

'Awkwardly' was an understatement, Annie

thought, looking at the child's splinted arm propped on a pillow. It was a mess.

'Possible loss of consciousness for a moment, but they think he might have fainted. GCS fifteen all the time we've been with him.' The paramedic reeled off the stats and the treatment to date, and they transferred him to the resus bed and introduced themselves.

While Ed checked him over and calmly issued instructions, Annie took the mother to one side and talked to her for a moment, calming her down and trying to reassure her before going back to Oliver's side.

He was trying so hard not to cry, but he had to be in significant pain. Frankly, that arm was enough to make the toughest of men cry, she thought, and he was just a little boy.

There was no sign of a head injury, no bumps or bruises or other indications, but they were still waiting for the X-rays and in the meantime his arm was their concern.

'How's the pulse in his wrist?' she asked softly, and Ed met her eyes across the child's body.

'Weak,' he murmured. 'Where are the orthos?'

'Coming, I think. Ah, here's the radiographer.'

The pictures spoke for themselves. The bones above and below the elbow joint were all fractured, the tip of the elbow had been sheared off and it was going to take some very skilled surgery to put him back together.

'Right, send that to the orthopaedic surgeon on call and say I want him down here stat,' Ed said crisply, just as the door swung open.

'Hi. You've got a query fractured arm for me?'

'I don't think there's a query,' Ed said drily, and flicked through all the views on the screen.

'Well, isn't it a good job I like jigsaws?' the surgeon said, wincing, and turned to the family. 'Hi, there. Oliver, is it? And are you his mother?'

'Yes.'

He was swiftly assessed for surgery and shipped out in the company of the nurse, leaving them alone with nothing between them but air that was filled with tension.

Ed met her eyes and his lips flickered in a wicked smile. 'Well, hi, Dr Brooks,' he murmured. 'How are you today?'

She smiled back, suddenly shy as the memory

of what they'd done last night flooded through her. 'I'm fine. I thought I'd better come and do something with you. Kate thought we'd had a row.' She gave him a wry smile. 'Apparently we've done too good a job of keeping our distance.'

He gave a slightly raw laugh. 'OK. Well, do you think we've passed the test?'

'I have no idea. I hope so.'

'Time for coffee?'

'Love one. Is that going too far?'

'Hell, no. We can have coffee, Annie. We just can't grope each other on the bench.'

Her eyes widened, then she started to laugh. 'You are so rude.'

'I'd like to be. Come on, before that damn phone rings.'

They took it to their usual spot, and he sat with his elbows on his knees and the paper cup dangling between them from his fingers, and she didn't have a clue what he was thinking. Oh, well, only one way to find out.

'Penny for them,' she said, and he turned his head and gave her a wry smile.

'I was just thinking if I sat like this long enough maybe my body would start to behave itself.'

She felt her nipples spring to attention. 'Well, that'll teach you to talk about groping me on the bench.'

'Won't it just?' He sat back, crossed one leg over the other knee and took a mouthful of coffee. 'So, since our minds are clearly on the subject, when are you free next?'

She felt her jaw sag slightly as heat shot through her, and shut her mouth fast. 'Um—not tonight, Mum's got something on, and tomorrow she's got book club—that's every Wednesday, so they're all out. Thursday my grandmother's coming over for supper and we're going to watch a film together.'

'Friday?'

She nodded, thinking it sounded like for ever, but there was no way they could meet up sooner and she didn't want to get in too deep too soon anyway. 'Friday I can do.'

'Thank goodness for that.' He sighed, and his

mouth twisted in a slight smile. 'I was beginning to wonder if you'd have to wash your hair.'

'Ed, I'm not making excuses,' she said, shaking her head. 'I'm really sorry it's so long, but at least from my mother's point of view it won't look suspiciously like we're properly seeing each other, and I can always make it sound like a group of colleagues going out. It has been known. If it's any consolation,' she added, going for broke because it was a little late for any pretence at reluctance, 'I'd happily make it tonight.'

She heard the suck of his breath, then a muttered oath. 'Why? Why tell me that here, now, when there's nothing we can do about it?'

She laughed softly. 'Because I didn't want you to think I wasn't interested?'

'I think we proved that one already,' he said drily. 'On both sides.'

'Yeah. Maybe we did.'

'No maybe about it. Sheesh, Annie, this is going to be so tough.'

She shook her head, a curious feeling of disappointment washing over her as she mentally scanned their rotas. Disappointment she hastily crushed. 'Well, if it's any help I'm not working tomorrow, I'm working on Thursday and you're off then, and neither of us are on duty on Friday, so it's only today we've got to deal with. We should be able to cope with that.'

Except that meant he wouldn't see her again for days, and he was shocked at the stab of disappointment that realisation brought with it.

'Probably as well,' he said, suddenly troubled by how deep in he seemed to have got already.

It's just physical. It doesn't mean anything, just that she's hot and you want more than just one night.

But it wasn't that. Or at least, not just that. And that *was* troubling. Very troubling. Damn.

'Time to go,' he said abruptly, and necked his coffee and went, leaving Annie sitting on the bench slightly open-mouthed and wondering what she'd missed.

Maybe he was miffed that she wasn't more readily available, that maybe he should have gone for Kate after all? And then she wouldn't be feeling like this, so desperate to spend time with him that Friday seemed light years away.

She was getting in too deep. She'd thought she could have fun, but maybe she wasn't strong enough, and maybe a little more distance this week would be good for them both.

She finished her coffee and followed him, but she made sure that for the rest of the day they weren't working together.

Better safe than sorry…

Friday crawled round.

The days seemed endless, divided between work and his grandparents' house, dealing with the fallout of his grandfather's relentless deterioration, and as for the nights…

The nights were hell on wheels.

He was on duty on Wednesday night, which was a relief because he didn't have to spend the night lying awake with a throbbing groin and the ridiculous urge to go round to her house and climb in the window and bury himself in her before he went mad.

But on Thursday morning, of course, she came on duty as he was going off, and he had to hand over the patients to her.

'I'll see you tomorrow,' she said as he was leaving, and he nodded curtly.

'Yeah. I'm looking forward to it.'

His smile felt tight, but she just smiled back, recognition of his frustration in her eyes, and she gave him the tiniest wink before she turned away.

Hell's teeth.

He went home, went to bed, then got up again, because clearly he wasn't going to sleep, and put on his running gear. He cut up past the hospital, out on the lanes into the open country and picked up the river wall to the harbour, then slowed to a walk and carried on along the sea wall, up the steps to the top and across the clifftop car park near his grandparents' house.

He was hot and sweaty, but he'd have a drink with them, check that everything was OK and then borrow the car and go home to shower and change and then come back. Maybe even take them out for lunch—except the way Grumps had been lately, that was unlikely.

They were in the garden, and Marnie greeted him with a smile and went to hug him.

'I shouldn't touch me, if I were you. I've been running, I'm pretty rancid,' he warned with a laugh. 'How's it going?'

'Oh, good today. Ed's here, darling.'

His grandfather looked up. 'Edward. Been ages. Too busy, I suppose.'

Ages? He shook his hand. 'I've been around, Grumps. How are you today?'

'Oh, all right. Stupid legs and things. Marnie, get drinks. Gin and tonic.'

'Ned, it's only eleven-thirty! You don't have your gin and tonic until six.'

The old man frowned, his muscles slow to react. 'Sure?'

'Quite sure. And, anyway, I've made lemonade. You know you like my lemonade.'

'I'll get it,' Ed said, leaving Marnie to deal with him. She'd perfected the art of distraction, and it usually worked like a charm.

He rejoined them a few minutes later, and all was tranquil again. 'Here—I found some biscuits, too.'

'He won't eat his lunch if he has biscuits,' Marnie murmured, but he shrugged.

'It doesn't matter. He hardly eats anything now. He just needs calories.'

'Well, I don't,' she muttered, rolling her eyes, and he chuckled and shook his head.

'You're lovely. Have half a biscuit. I'll have the other half.'

'Only if I let you,' she said with a laugh.

He stayed with them for an hour, then borrowed the car, drove home and showered and went back for the rest of the day. He'd had in mind taking his grandfather out for a push along the prom, but Marnie needed to go shopping, so he stayed with him and tackled some of the gardening while his grandfather dozed in the shade.

'I tell you what,' Marnie said after she came back. 'The forecast for tomorrow is good, too. If you aren't too busy, why don't we go down to the beach hut in the morning?'

Because he'd been going to get the house ready for Annie, but what, realistically, was there to get ready? The bed?

Don't think about the bed.

'That sounds good. I'll come over first thing to give you a hand, and then we can go down as soon as we're ready. There might be some sailing boats out there for him to watch.'

'Thank you. I do appreciate it and he will, too, even if he doesn't show it,' she said, going up on tiptoe and kissing his cheek. 'You need a shave,' she scolded, but he just grinned.

'I never shave on my days off. It's part of my bad-boy image.'

She tutted and smacked his hand, and he laughed and hugged her. 'Right, I'm off. I'll see you later, at bedtime.'

'Are you sure?'

'Sure I'm sure. It's a pleasure.'

'Now I know you're lying.'

He couldn't help the wry laugh. 'OK, then. It's a privilege. Is that better?'

'Oh, Ed…' She caught her breath and hugged him fiercely. 'You're such a good man. You should be married, with children.'

Pain slammed into him, taking him by surprise. 'Marnie, I haven't got time in my life for that,' he said gruffly, 'and anyway, I've never met a woman I'd want to spend my life with.'

Until now.

And where the hell had *that* come from?

He kissed her goodbye and left, walking swiftly away from her less-than-subtle innuendo and loving interference, but he couldn't outrun Annie, it seemed. The house was full of her, and, exhausted though he was, he couldn't just crawl into bed and sleep for a few hours because the bed had become the biggest memory-magnet of them all.

He went into the sitting room, about the only room in the house she hadn't been in, and fell asleep in the corner of the sofa, waking with a crick in his neck to the sound of the phone ringing.

It was Marnie.

'Darling, I just wondered when you were coming, because Ned's getting a bit restless.'

He blinked at his watch, swore silently and scraped a hand through his hair.

'Ah—um, I'll come now. Sorry. I sat down for a minute. I must have dropped off. I'll be right with you.'

He stood up, stretched out the kinks and without allowing himself to think about it he got back on the merry-go-round.

'Can we go to the beach, Mummy? Pleeeeeee-ase?'

'And can we take the buckets and spades and make a sandcastle?'

The beach? What a good idea. It was a glorious day, and the beach would be perfect. She grinned at the girls. 'Why not? You get the toys out of the sandpit, and I'll find your swimming things. Shall we take a picnic?'

'Yay! Can we have cheese and pickle sandwiches?'

'And cherry tomatoes and grapes and chocolate biscuits—'

'I don't think we can take chocolate biscuits on a hot day,' she pointed out, laughing, and pushed them both gently towards the door. 'Shoo. Go and get the buckets and spades or the sun will have gone by the time you've finished talking about it.'

'Is MamaJo coming?'

She looked at her mother. 'Mum?'

'I don't know. Go and get your things and I'll think about it.'

The girls tumbled out of the patio door, and Annie searched her mother's eyes. 'You don't have to. If you want time to yourself, I'm quite happy to take them on my own.'

'Are you? I've got a new book to read and I'd love a quiet hour or two. I might come down later. Are you going to take the windbreak?'

'Probably. I'm going to drive, so we can go to the nice bit of beach near the cliff. There's a café there and an ice-cream kiosk and loos, so it's really handy.' Not to mention close to where Ed's grandparents lived, so she could eye up the houses and speculate…

Her mother nodded. 'OK. I'll read for a while, and come down and join you later if I get bored. Don't forget your phone. And suncream.'

'As if,' she said, rolling her eyes and throwing the picnic together. Twenty minutes later they were out of the door, all three of them in their costumes and beach dresses and sunhats, the picnic and sandpit toys were in the car and they were on their way.

It really was a fabulous day, the warmest day yet this year, and although the sea would probably be too cold the beach would be lovely, and it would be fun building sandcastles with the girls. Relaxing.

She could do with something relaxing, because it was Friday, and that meant—she checked her watch—less than twelve hours to her secret tryst with Ed. Her heart thumped at the thought, her senses leaping into life.

The suspense was going to kill her!

She pulled into the clifftop car park, facing the houses that looked out across the car park at the sea beyond. They were interesting houses. Some had been built in the thirties, all curved glass and gun-emplacement architecture, others were newer, with a modernist feel, and all of them were highly desirable.

So which…?

'Mummy, come on!'

The girls were bouncing in their seats, and she was behaving like a crazy stalker. She pulled herself together, loaded them up with as much as they could carry, grabbed the cool bag, the windbreak and everything else and struggled down the steps to the beach. They found a spot midway between the bottom of the steps and the café, by which time her shoulder was screaming from the weight of all the apparently necessary equipment that was hanging from it.

'This'll do fine,' she said in relief, and while she set up the windbreak and found the sun-cream, the girls stripped off and started to dig.

She smothered them in factor fifty, taking particular care with Grace with her fairer skin, gave herself a squirt of factor twenty and settled down on her towel with a book while the girls amused themselves building a sandcastle.

She'd help if they asked, but it was too easy to take over and there were already two of them squabbling about who was doing it best without her sticking her oar in.

In the end she had to intervene, and with a sigh she put her book away and went and joined them. 'Why don't we dig a moat all round the outside and you can fill it with water?' she suggested, and they spent the next ten minutes digging it and then got their feet cold and wet, fetching water from the sea.

The girls shrieked and ran back, laughing, leaving Annie to scoop up the water, and of course the hem of her dress got wet and then as she was turning away she stumbled and another wave came and drenched her while she was on her knees.

'Oh! It's freezing!' she wailed, and the girls giggled and jumped up and down gleefully. 'Little horrors. It's mean to laugh,' she said, trailing soggily back to the sandcastle with water streaming off her dress and running down her legs.

'You should have taken it off, Mummy, like us, and then it wouldn't be wet,' Grace said sagely, and Annie sighed. Clever child. And of course she would have taken it off if it wasn't for the fact that the costume was an old one she'd had before the girls, and it was a bit on the snug side at the top end. Well, both ends, really. So much for her modesty. She peeled off the thin cotton sundress and hung it over the windbreak.

'You're quite right. I tell you what, while it dries, why don't we go and get an ice-cream?'

Only of course nothing ever worked quite according to plan. The girls ran ahead, not paying attention as usual, and Grace tripped up the steps and fell hard onto her hands and knees on the sandy concrete surface of the prom.

She burst into tears, and Annie knelt down beside her and hugged her. 'Oh, darling—are you all right?' she asked, but Grace was sobbing and blood was already oozing from both knees and one of her hands.

'It h-ur-rts,' she wailed, and Annie hugged her and rocked her while Chloe patted her shoulder and made soothing noises and looked worried to bits.

'It's OK, she's all right,' Annie reassured her, but Grace shook her head.

'Not a-all ri-ight,' she sobbed, and burrowed into Annie's shoulder.

Typical. The first-aid kit was in the car, Grace was beside herself and she was too heavy to carry that far.

She lifted her head a fraction and there, right

in front of her, were bare feet. Strong, masculine feet, topped by well-muscled legs sticking out of a pair of faded board shorts.

There was a scar on the left knee, a scar she'd seen only the other night, and she felt relief flood through her.

He'd been watching them for a while.

Not deliberately, but they'd been right in front of him and it was hard not to. Especially when she fell in the sea and then had to strip off.

Voyeur.

But then he'd seen the accident happen and he'd had to go and help. Not that he wanted to interfere, and they were supposed to be keeping their families out of it, but he couldn't just sit there and ignore them while the child sobbed her heart out.

'Annie? Can I do anything?'

He crouched down, reaching out a hand to touch her arm, and she closed her eyes and bit her lip.

'Grace fell over. She's only skinned her knees and hands, but my first-aid kit's in the car.'

He gave a resigned but silent sigh. So much for keeping them all apart. 'No problem. We've got one in the beach hut. Come on.'

Chloe let go of her sister, he helped Annie to her feet with Grace still in her arms and took them to the beach hut just a few yards away, where his grandparents were sitting watching.

'Here we go. Marnie, Grumps, this is Annie. She's a friend of mine, and her little girl's just fallen over and cut her knees.'

'And my hand,' Grace sniffed, making sure they knew the full extent of her injuries.

'Oh, dear,' Marnie said comfortingly, rising to the occasion as she always did. 'Well, now, I'm sure there's something we can do about that. I think there's some boiled water in the kettle. It should be cool enough to use. Do you want some salt in it, Ed?'

'Please. Here, Annie, sit down and let's have a look at the invalid, shall we?'

He shoved a little folding beach chair her way, and she sat down with a plop, as if her legs had given way. He crouched down in front of them and smiled at Grace. 'Hiya, Grace. My name's

Ed, and I work with your mummy. Shall we see if I can make your cuts better?'

She glanced up at her mother, checking, and Annie smiled and brushed the halo of curls back off her face.

'Ed's a children's doctor,' she told her daughter seriously. 'He's very, very good.'

'Will it hurt?'

'Well, now, it might a little,' he told her honestly, 'but it'll feel much better after the sand's washed out and we've put some nice cream on.'

'Are you going to put ice cream on it?' Chloe asked, looking confused, and he chuckled.

'*Nice* cream, not ice cream,' he corrected, smiling at her. 'But maybe if you're good we can get you all an ice cream afterwards, if Mummy says yes.'

'We were going to get an ice cream,' Grace told him, watching him warily as he squeezed out a gauze swab and dabbed the first knee. 'Ow!'

'Sorry, sweetheart. I tell you what, why don't you grab hold of my hair and if it gets really bad, you can pull it hard. OK?'

'OK.'

He felt the little fingers grasp a lock just over his temple, and winced. She already had a death grip on it. What it would be like if he hurt her? Oh, well, no doubt he'd survive.

'OK, here we go.' He swabbed gently, but the tug on his scalp didn't change, and he finished both knees and then looked at her hands, sighing quietly with relief when she let go of his hair. One palm needed a quick swipe, but the grazes were all clean, there was no sand embedded in any of them, luckily, and once they were protected by plasters he sat back on his heels and grinned at her.

'Brave girl. I definitely think that deserves an ice cream, don't you, Mummy?'

'I think so,' she said, her smile rueful and her eyes filled with gratitude. 'Thank you, Ed.'

'You're welcome.'

'Aren't you going to kiss it better?' Chloe asked him. 'Mummy always kisses us better if we get an owie.'

'Well, maybe we'd better let Mummy do it, if it's her job,' he said, jackknifing to his feet and taking a step back. 'I tell you what, why don't we go and get the ice creams, and Mummy and Grace can stay here and have a cuddle. OK?'

Anything rather than crouching there looking down the gaping cleavage of Annie's swimming costume.

Annie rummaged in her bag for her purse. 'Here, Ed, take some money—'

'Don't be ridiculous.' She opened her mouth to protest, but he ignored her and looked down at her now happier daughter. 'What would you like, Grace?'

'Can I have one of those squishy ones with the chocolate in it?'

'A ninety-nine? It's OK by me, that's what I'm going to have. Annie?'

She gave up the unequal struggle and smiled at him. 'Ditto. Thank you.'

'You're welcome. Marnie?'

'No, darling. You take Chloe and get the ice creams. I'll put the kettle on, and we can all have tea and get to know each other.'

He hesitated for a moment, torn between honouring his promise to the girls and the danger of leaving Annie alone with Marnie, but he would be gone only moments. Realistically, what harm could come of it? He shrugged and looked at Chloe. 'Coming?'

'Yup.' She skipped up to him and threaded her hand in his, and after a heartbeat he tightened his grip and set off towards the kiosk.

CHAPTER SIX

ANNIE WATCHED THEM go, a lump in her throat. The trusting way Chloe had gone to him, the way she'd taken his hand—and they were supposed to be keeping their families out of this!

She'd been so relieved to see him when Grace had fallen over that the implications of him riding to the rescue on his white charger had gone straight over her head.

Not now. Damn.

And talking of families, she turned belatedly to his grandmother and smiled, holding out her hand.

'I'm so sorry about the intrusion. We haven't really been introduced. I'm Annie Brooks. Ed and I work together.'

Marnie took her hand but, instead of shaking it, she squeezed it gently in both of hers. 'I know. It's nice to meet you, Annie, I've heard a lot about you. I'm Julia, really, but everyone calls me Marnie. And this is Ned.'

He was slightly behind her and to one side, and as Annie shifted in her chair and turned to look at him properly for the first time, she felt her smile falter. He was in a wheelchair, which she'd expected from what little Ed had told her, but it was the stiffness of his body, the slow lifting of his hand and the remoteness in his eyes that stopped her in her tracks as everything toppled gently into place.

So that was it. The reason Ed was so wary of relationships, so determined not to settle, so driven by his career. The reason this man for whom family was so important didn't seem to want a family of his own? Because he—?

She felt the shock wave right down to her bones, and it was a second before she caught herself and dredged up a proper smile. 'Hello, Ned,' she said, her voice a little over-bright. 'I'm Annie.'

His words were slurred. 'Do I know you?'

She shook her head. 'No. We've never met, but Ed talks very fondly of you.'

'Ed?'

'Edward, darling. Stephen's boy.'

'Well, say Edward.'

Marnie met her eyes with an apologetic smile. 'Ignore that, please, it's not a good day today,' she said softly, and perched on a chair next to Annie. 'So, Grace,' she said with a big smile, 'are you the oldest or the youngest?'

'I'm the oldest but Chloe doesn't listen to me, she's naughty.'

Annie chuckled and hugged her close. 'Not always. And you can be naughty, too.'

Marnie laughed. 'All children are naughty. It's healthy. Ed was the most mischievous child I've ever met, but he's turned into the kindest and most dependable man you could ever wish to meet.'

She met Annie's eyes, the subtext clear, and it was only the piercing whistle of the kettle on the little gas ring in the back of the beach hut that broke her gaze.

'Tea, Annie?'

But she could see Ed approaching, had seen him all but flinch when Chloe had slipped her hand in his, and she thought they'd probably intruded enough. Not to mention the hero-worship she could see in Chloe's eyes. And now she knew the truth, there was no way she was letting her children get involved with him. Panic swamped her and she had to crush it down.

'No, thank you, Marnie. I'll just have the ice cream. We've got a sandcastle to finish before the tide comes in and swallows it.'

'Oh, well, never mind. Perhaps another time? Then we can have a proper chat.'

She nearly laughed out loud. Not if she could avoid it, and there was no way her mother and Marnie were *ever* going to get together. They were far too alike and she could just imagine the conversation and the ensuing interrogation. So much for all that privacy they'd talked about on Monday!

'That would be lovely,' she said, crossing her fingers as Grace wriggled off her lap and ran to meet Ed and Chloe. Pity. Having Grace on her lap had acted like a shield to hide behind, and now Ed's eyes were raking over her body in the inadequate little black one-piece and she wanted to run away, her thoughts in turmoil.

'Hi, there,' she said, getting to her feet to start the process of escaping. 'Is that mine?'

He smiled innocently. 'It is. I had to lick it, it was starting to melt and dribble down the cone. You wouldn't want it to get soggy.'

She could see the mark of his tongue all around the base of the pale creamy spiral where it met the sugar cone, and his eyes twinkled at her over the top. So much for innocence.

'I had to lick Grace's,' Chloe told her, breaking the thread that held their gazes locked.

'Did you? That was kind.'

'You can't have it, it's mine,' Grace said, taking it from her sister in case she lost any more.

'Careful, mind you don't drop it. Girls, say thank you to Ed.'

'Thank you for my ice cream,' they chorused, and he smiled at them.

'My pleasure. How are the knees, Grace?'

'Better now. Mummy, can we go and finish the sandcastle?'

She heaved a silent sigh of relief. 'Good idea.

We'll get out of your hair. Thank you for the rescue mission. I'm sorry we invaded your privacy.'

'Don't be silly,' Marnie said, emerging from the beach hut and smiling warmly at her. 'You're welcome to join us any time.'

Not if he had anything to say about it, Annie was sure, and not if she did either, but she thanked his grandmother anyway, waved to his grandfather and then turned back to Ed. 'Thank you, too. For the first aid, for the ice creams. It was very kind of you.'

'Any time.' His eyes held hers again. 'I'll see you at nine,' he murmured softly, and she nodded.

'Yes.'

Then his eyes slid down her body, back up to her face and his lips shifted into a mischievous smile he'd probably been perfecting since before he'd learned to walk.

'I'll look forward to it.'

She turned away before her legs melted like the ice cream, and ran her tongue round the same spot that he'd licked just moments before.

Me, too, but at some point we have a lot to discuss. Like why you haven't told me what's really wrong with your grandfather, and what it means for you...

She was aware of his presence in every cell of her body.

Every time she glanced up through her lashes, he was there, watching her surreptitiously. It made her feel oddly self-conscious, but also curiously comforted.

She guessed Marnie would be giving him the third degree, and she just hoped her mother didn't turn up any time soon to add fuel to the fire, because she was more sure than ever now that this relationship was going nowhere.

She didn't come, but the next time Annie looked up, the hut was closed and they'd gone. And she felt bereft.

Stupid. So stupid. This was no-strings, just an affair, a little light recreational sex to add another dimension to their lives. She didn't need to feel *bereft*, for goodness' sake, just because he'd gone!

But she did, and the rest of the day stretched out in front of them like a yawning void. It was still hours before she'd see him again, hours before she could ask him the questions that were burning a hole in her. Hours before she could hold him—

'There's MamaJo!' Chloe cried, and she felt a surge of relief. Something to take her mind off Ed, she thought, but of course it didn't work like that.

'Oh, Grace, what happened to your knees, darling?' her mother asked, and then it all poured out and of course Ed's name came up.

Out of the mouths of babes, Annie thought wryly.

'Well, how lucky he was here,' her mother said, and then looked up and caught her eye. 'Or had you arranged to meet?'

It took a huge effort not to look away. 'No. It was just a fortunate coincidence.'

'Hmm,' her mother said, as if she didn't believe a word.

And that was the end of any semblance of privacy.

* * *

The gates were open when she arrived a moment after nine, but his car wasn't there.

Maybe he'd parked it somewhere else, she thought, and ducked through the wisteria curtain into the garden proper just as he reversed the car in. She went back out to the carport as he unfolded himself from the driver's seat and straightened up.

'Hi, there.'

He turned to her, ran a hand through his hair and smiled distractedly.

'Hi. Sorry, I was a bit on the drag. Have you been waiting long?'

'No, you're fine, I've only just arrived.'

'Good. I left the gates open for you in case I was held up.'

His voice was low, and it wrapped around her like the scented garden. He brushed past her, shutting the gates, and then turned to her with a slow, sexy smile that made her toes curl. She went up on tiptoe and brushed her lips against his, but apparently that wasn't enough. He caught her against his body, threaded his fingers through her hair and kissed her properly.

Improperly?

Whatever, she was more than happy for him to kiss her, to hold her, to give her a chance to hold him after the past few hours of tumbling thoughts.

He slowly pulled away, ending the kiss with a soft sigh that drifted over her face, and let her go, dropping his hands to her hips and looking down at her with that lazy, sexy smile playing around his mouth. 'Oh, that's better. I needed that. It's been ages.'

'What, since this morning?' she teased, keeping it light for now, and he laughed.

'No. Since I kissed you on Monday. Come on, I've got some wine in the fridge with our names on it.' He slid an arm round her shoulders and steered her under the arch into the garden and through to the house. 'How's Grace?'

'Bit sore, but she'll be fine. Thank you so much for your help.'

'No probs. It was a pleasure. They're lovely kids.'

'They are,' she said softly. 'They're the best thing that's ever happened to me, and I'd move heaven and earth to protect them, but you can't always prevent them from getting hurt.' And then, since they were talking about relatives, she went on with her voice carefully neutral, 'How's your grandfather? Did you have a good day after you left?'

'Oh, he's fine. He slept most of the afternoon, he was a bit tired. All that fresh air.' He straightened up from the fridge, wine bottle in hand, and eyed her thoughtfully. 'You've caught the sun,' he said, changing the subject, and she let it drop. For now.

'The curse of fair skin.'

He smiled and ran the pad of one thumb over her cheek, sending a tingle through her. 'Your freckles have come out.'

'Always. First sign of summer, out they pop. And before you ask, yes, I wear factor fifteen moisturiser every day and put on sunscreen. And the kids were smothered.'

He laughed. 'Good. Take this,' he said, handing her the wine bottle, and led her back out to the garden, a tray full of goodies in his hands.

'Sit down, make yourself comfortable. I need to chill for a bit.'

'That's fine. I'm more than happy to sit here. It's a lovely garden and the company's all right.'

'Only all right?'

'Are you fishing for compliments?'

'Would I?' His grin was wry and touched with mischief as he handed her a glass of the perfectly chilled sauvignon blanc, and she sipped it appreciatively, snagging one of the lovely olive breadsticks that he'd brought out, too.

'Oh, that's good,' she said, sighing contentedly and settling back in the chair. 'Perfect end to a gorgeous day. It was fabulous on the beach—well, injuries aside. I'm really sorry we invaded your personal space, but I'm just so glad you were there because my first-aid kit was in the car and it would have been an ergonomic nightmare otherwise.'

'That's the handy thing about the beach hut. Home from home, and you don't have to lug all that stuff. It makes a day on the beach so much easier.'

'Oh, I can see how that would work. Getting

all the stuff down there is like a polar expedition, and getting it back is worse. Do you often use it?'

A little frown creased his brow, but so fleetingly if she hadn't been watching him she would have missed it. 'Not so much now. We used to, all the time. They've had it for ever. Now we only go down there when Grumps is up to it, which is increasingly rare. You should borrow it. I can let you have a key, I'm sure Marnie won't mind. It's standing idle and the girls would enjoy it.'

'But what if your grandfather's having a good day? Won't they be there?'

He shook his head. 'Not if I'm at work. Marnie can't manage the hill with his wheelchair. I'll talk to her tomorrow. And we need to move the playhouse for you. She reminded me about it after you went back to your sandcastle.'

'Really? Oh, Ed, I thought it was just an idle suggestion, or I would have thanked them.'

'Of course it wasn't idle. You're welcome to it. You can have it as soon as you like.'

She frowned. 'I don't know how, though. Even in bits it won't go in my car.'

'No probs. Grumps has got a trailer it'll go in, and a car with a tow hitch. If it'll go through the side gate, we don't even have to take it apart. Measure it, let me know. Here.'

He picked up a breadstick and leant over the table, holding the end out to her. She bit it, and he turned it round, closed his lips around it and bit off the end. The end that had touched her lips. Just like the ice-cream cone that had sent her into meltdown earlier in the day. And then he turned it back to her, his eyes curiously intent. She parted her lips to take it, and felt the tension in the garden ramp up to a whole new level.

The time for small talk was over.

What *was* it about him?

Not technique, although he was certainly no slouch in that department, but he didn't even have to touch her and she was on fire. Just a glance—not even that. The mere thought was enough to take her to the edge.

She'd never been so in tune with another person in her life, and yet there was so little she knew about him. Maybe she didn't need to know any more? Although there were things she *did* know, which he hadn't told her. Things they needed to discuss?

'OK?'

The word was a low rumble against her ear, and she shifted her head against his shoulder, tilting it back so she could meet his eyes. They were languid, but even now in the background was a latent heat. She tried not to smile.

'Actually, no. That was rubbish.'

He chuckled and tilted her head a little more and kissed her. 'Liar,' he growled softly.

'Mmm.' She smiled against his lips, and then rested her head back on his shoulder and gave a quiet sigh.

'What is it?'

How to say it? She ran her fingers over his chest, feeling the definition of his muscles under the sprinkling of dark hair. He was fit. Strong. Powerful. And articulate, his acute intelligence and razor wit an important part of who he was. But for how long?

She propped herself up on one elbow so she could read him better, because she knew her next words were going to have repercussions, but they had to be said.

Carefully, her voice soft and non-confrontational, she said quietly, 'How long has your grandfather had Huntington's disease?'

Every cell in his body froze.

Damn.

'Did Marnie tell you?'

'No. I'm a doctor, Ed. I looked at him. One glance was enough.'

Of course it was. She wasn't stupid. He turned his head, staring blankly across the room, and swallowed hard.

'Ed? Talk to me.'

'There's nothing to say.'

'Isn't there? Or is it just that you don't want to say it?'

He turned back to her again, knowing he was angry, knowing she'd read it in his eyes, but she held her ground and touched his face with gentle fingers.

'Have you inherited the gene from your grandfather?'

Trust her to go for the bloody jugular.

'No.' Not from his grandfather.

'So it's not because of the threat of HD that you don't want kids, don't want to get married, don't want a relationship worth diddly-squat?'

His heart pounded. Should he lie to her? It was none of her damn business, and he could tell her that, or lie, or just refuse to discuss it. But for some reason that he simply couldn't fathom, he *wanted* to talk to her.

Could he trust her with the truth?

Yes. She had no axe to grind, no interest in a permanent relationship, no desire to get involved ever again with a man in that way. She'd said as much already, told him in words of one syllable that she'd move heaven and earth to protect her girls, and that meant not exposing them to risk of any sort.

And he was a risk.

He was an unexploded bomb, and the clock was ticking. What he didn't know was if it would ever detonate or if it was just a dummy.

'It's not that simple,' he said eventually.

Her voice was gentle. 'I didn't for a moment think it would be.'

'No. I mean, it's *really* not that simple. I don't know how much you know about HD.'

'Some. I know it's inherited, and I know it's not gender linked, so either sex can develop it. I know you can have genetic counselling and screening and it's a long and involved process. I know the age of onset tends to decrease as it goes down the generations, and I know what it does to the body and the mind as it destroys part of the brain, and the destructive impact the threat of it has on families.'

He nodded. He lived with that threat every day of his life. Destructive? She had no idea.

'And I know it's a mutation of the huntingtin gene on one of the chromosomes,' she added. 'That's all I can remember.'

He nodded. 'OK. Well, everyone has the gene, but what causes the disease is when that gene mutates. Think of a string of beads, all different colours, and every bead is a different gene that gives us different characteristics like hair colour and so on. With HD, it's like having several beads of the same colour in a row, and the more you have, the more likely you are to get the symptoms. And when it's handed down, because it's not the most stable gene when it's copied, it can be inclined to mutate and expand so you get more beads, as it were. It almost never decreases. The average is about eighteen. Under twenty six, you're fine. That's normal. Over forty, you'll definitely develop symptoms at some point in your life if you live long enough, and the higher the number, the longer the string of identical beads, if you like, the earlier the onset of the symptoms. Still with me?'

She nodded, and he continued, 'My grandfather has forty-two, which is why he only got it nine years ago, and he's the first person in his family to develop it, but he didn't pass it on.'

Her brows tugged together in a little frown. 'So—your father didn't inherit the gene?'

'Yes, but not from Grumps. He only has thirty-four repeats, and, as I said, it doesn't tend to decrease over the generations. So they looked at

Marnie, and found she'd got thirty-four repeats, too, so it came from her.'

'Marnie?' She sounded shocked. 'So—will she..?' She trailed off, and he shook his head.

'No. Between twenty-six and forty is a grey area, with the risk increasing as the number rises. You're safe right up to the mid-thirties, and after that the risk increases, but even if you're safe yourself, when you pass it on the gene can expand. So Marnie herself is safe.'

'She'll never develop the symptoms?'

'No, and nor will my father, not if he lives to be a hundred, but the gene is unstable when it's handed down the male line. That's when it's most likely to expand, and if it expands enough, you cop it.'

He could feel her eyes on him, the intense concentration of her gaze, the comfort of her touch as her hand lay against his pounding heart, the thumb moving slowly, rhythmically, soothing him.

'And?' she asked softly.

She wasn't going to give up, was she? But she might as well know it all. Know the truth, know why he was so determined never to have a family of his own.

'I don't know,' he told her, his voice raw, and he felt the slight intake of her breath in the shift of her ribs against his side. 'I had the counselling, we all did. That was after Grumps was diagnosed and my father's repeats didn't match and they'd traced it to Marnie. We all went for the counselling and testing, and my brother and aunt are fine. My aunt wanted to know if she'd handed it on, and so did my brother, because his wife was pregnant with their second child.'

'And you?' she coaxed, when he hesitated.

'I took the test, but when it came to it I realised I didn't want to know the result. I don't know if I have it, how many repeats I have, if it's expanded at all from my father to me, or not enough to make me certain of developing it at any point in the future. I wouldn't let them tell me that. I just know there's a fifty-fifty chance I've inherited it, and if I have, even if it hasn't expanded, even if *I'm* safe, I can never take the risk of handing it on to future generations, which is why I've decided never to have children, because I'm not handing this damn disease on to ruin any more lives. It stops with me. And that's not negotiable.'

She was silent for so long that he turned his head to look at her. Her eyes were trained on him, and tears shimmered in their clouded blue depths. 'I'm so sorry,' she said softly. 'That must have been such a tough decision to make.'

'Not really. It doesn't honestly make very much difference to me. My brother's in the clear, he's got three kids, so the family name won't die out, my parents have grandchildren so that box is ticked—and that's me off the hook as far as the whole happy-ever-after thing goes. I don't want to have to watch some poor woman buckle under the strain like Marnie is. I couldn't do that to anyone, never mind someone I loved as much as Grumps loved Marnie. He'd be devastated if he understood the impact this is having on her, but he had no idea it was on the cards until it was too late, and now his emotions are skewed and he doesn't care or even realise.

'But it's not too late for me, because there's nobody in my life to get hurt by my decision, and there never will be. This way I can do what I want, live my life how I choose—'

'Can you, though?' she asked, and although her voice was still gentle, her question wasn't and it went right to the heart of the argument his brother had used on him time and time again. 'Can you really? Surely you're just denying yourself the potential opportunity to have a lifetime of happiness in a loving relationship on the strength of a mere possibility—is that really what you choose, or are you just running from the truth?'

Damn. He couldn't take this. The room was closing in on him, the insidious fear that had been a part of his life for nine years now rising up and choking him.

'I don't want to talk about this anymore,' he said, and, throwing back the covers, he got out of bed, picked up his clothes and left the room.

Annie lay there in the tangle of bedding and stared at the empty doorway until it blurred.

She'd convinced herself today that he'd got the gene, that he was going to disintegrate like his grandfather, and when she'd realised he didn't necessarily have it, she'd expected to feel relief, but all she felt was the crushing weight of uncertainty.

How could he live like that, with so many unknowns? Well, only one, really. Would he or wouldn't he die slowly by inches like his grandfather? And put like that, if the answer should turn out to be yes, why *would* he want to know, so it was hanging over him for the rest of his life? Not hanging over her, because she wasn't involved—was she?

Oh, hell.

She dropped back against the pillows and stared at the ceiling while tears trickled slowly out of the corners of her eyes and leaked down into her hair.

'Damn!' she whispered. 'Damn, damn, damn!'

And then she sniffed hard, swiped the tears off her temples with an impatient hand, pulled on her clothes and followed him. The last thing he needed was a pity party going on in his bedroom and, anyway, this wasn't about her, it was about him.

She found him in the garden, sitting in the gathering dark on the swing seat, a glass of wine in his hand. She walked over to him and put her hand on his shoulder, but he didn't move, and after a moment she went across to the table, picking up her empty glass.

'Any more in the bottle?'

The ice bucket was on the ground at his feet. He pushed it towards her, and she poured half a glass with a hand that was far from steady. Well, she'd known all day that this was on the cards, so she had no business being shocked, but the thought of it hanging over him, this young, fit man, so strong, so vital, so *alive*? It shocked her. To the core.

She sat down next to him, and the swing creaked and swayed a little before it came to rest.

Her voice was soft in the darkness. 'Will you ever find out?'

'No. If I'm getting it, it'll find me, and until then, I'm not going to borrow trouble.'

'And what do your family say?'

'They think I'm in the clear. Well, my brother knows I haven't found out, but nobody else.'

'You lied to them, in other words?'

'Not exactly. I told them I hadn't had a positive result.'

'And do they believe you?'

He shrugged. 'Dad does. He heaved a sigh of relief and went back to work. Business resumed.'

'And your mother?'

'Her, too.'

'And Marnie?'

The silence was telling, and she held her nerve and waited him out. After several tense seconds, he let out a sigh.

'I told her she'd never have to see me go through it. And that's not a lie, but she knows it's also not the truth, the whole truth and nothing but the truth, but I've never been able to lie to her, and whenever I tell her I'm OK and she won't ever have to see me like him, she says, "If you say so." And I can tell from her eyes that she doesn't believe a word of it.

'And that's the hardest bit,' he said, his voice fracturing momentarily. 'Lying to her. Knowing she wants me to find out the truth and set her mind at rest, so she knows she hasn't inadvertently handed me a death sentence. But I don't want to know, and it's my right not to know. If it was going to be, no, I don't have the gene, then of course I'd want to know. If it was going to be, yes, but it's not mutated any further, then it would be wise to know so that I didn't have children. But if I have it, and it's mutated, and I'll develop it at some point down the line, then I really, really don't want to know.

'I don't want to live my life watching and waiting, worried every time I drop something or trip over or can't remember someone's name, and once the result is delivered, once the words are said, they can't be unsaid.'

But you'll be thinking that anyway, all your life, waiting for a sign! You have to know! One way or the other, you have to know...

As if he could read her mind, he turned his head and met her eyes. 'It's my decision, Annie. No one else's. Please respect that.'

She swallowed hard and nodded. 'I do. And I wasn't trying to persuade you to get the result, I just wanted to understand how you'd come to the decision, and now I do, so thank you for telling me. I know it wasn't easy, and if you don't want to, we need never talk about it again.'

He searched her eyes in the gloom, and she heard a quiet sigh as some of the tension left him. 'Thank you.'

'And before you say it, I won't tell anyone.'

He inclined his head slightly in acknowledgement, and got to his feet. 'I'll walk you home.'

'Thank you.'

They didn't speak again, just walked silently through the quiet streets to her door, their fingers linked. She turned to say goodnight, but without a word he cupped her face in his hands and kissed her. It wasn't a tender kiss, and it wasn't passionate. It felt more like the signing of a pact, as if they'd moved into another phase of their relationship, and she supposed they had.

He could have lied, told her he didn't have the gene and left it at that, but he hadn't. He'd trusted her, and that meant more to her than he would ever know. She lifted her hand and touched his cheek, her fingertips grazing against the roughness of stubble on his jaw.

'Goodnight, Ed. I'll see you at work.'

He nodded, and still without speaking he turned and walked swiftly away.

Outrunning his demons?

Her heart ached for him, and for Marnie, who might never know the truth. Lord, what a nightmare. What a ghastly, insidious disease. And it might, in time, do to him what it had done to his grandfather.

Oh, God, no, not Ed. Not my Ed!

Pain stabbed through her, and blinking away the threatening tears she let herself quietly into the silent house.

He's not your Ed! It's not like that—it's just an affair! Don't go and spoil it all by falling in love with him!

But as she lay alone in her little bedroom, her own words echoing in her head, she knew it was too late for the warning, too late to remind herself of the rules, because she loved Ed Shackleton. Loved him in a way she'd never loved anyone, and it was the last thing on earth he'd want to hear.

He couldn't believe he'd told her.

He hadn't discussed it with a living soul apart

from the genetic counsellor and his brother, and that not for years. It was a no-go area, and his brother, for all he disagreed, respected that.

But it had dragged it all up to the surface again, and guilt racked him. Guilt for lying to Marnie, for not having the courage to find out the truth, for making her live in fear for him because he wanted to live in ignorance.

And ignorance, as he knew only too well, wasn't necessarily bliss.

He went home, cleared up the glasses in the garden and went to bed, but it smelled of Annie and he lay on his stomach with his face in her pillow, and breathed her in, and missed her…

CHAPTER SEVEN

BY THE MORNING, she'd pulled herself together.

She didn't want this, and she wasn't going to allow it to happen. Yes, he was a lovely guy, yes, she could easily let herself get all maudlin and ridiculous over him and start dreaming about happy ever after, but he'd made it clear he didn't want that, and anyway she knew only too well that it was all a myth, so she shut the lid firmly on the box, kissed the girls goodbye and went to work.

It was her turn to cover the weekend, and that meant working with Ed, so all the way there she lectured herself on her weakness for him. She needed distance, but how on earth could she achieve it? Less time spent with him at work, more time thinking about other things and not Ed, Ed, Ed, every waking moment. Exercise a little self-discipline.

And a more professional attitude at work.

She could do it. She could look him in the eye, smile and say hi without succumbing to that lazy smile or the smouldering message in those gorgeous slate-blue eyes.

She could.

She did. He was standing by the whiteboard, and she walked straight up to him, smiled and said, 'Hi. Ready for the day?'

His eyes searched hers, and his mouth quirked fleetingly as if he realised what she was doing. 'My day started three hours ago with a call from Marnie,' he said drily. 'Grumps fell out of bed.'

'Oh, no! Is he all right?' she asked, forgetting all about detachment.

He shrugged. 'So-so. Bit bruised, bit shaken up. I couldn't find anything worrying and I looked him over pretty thoroughly.'

'Does he need cot sides?'

The shrug again, a wry smile. 'Of course he does, but he's nothing if not stubborn. I'm just going to have to overrule him, but he'll hate it. He already hates sleeping downstairs without Marnie, so she's camping out in the sitting room.'

She felt a wave of empathy. She'd only spent a few moments with Marnie, but she'd really liked her and this was so tough on all of them.

'Oh, Ed. I'm really sorry. Can she go on like this?'

Something flickered in his eyes—desperation? She wasn't sure, and it was gone before she could analyse it, but then he gave a wry laugh. Not really a laugh. A little huff of sound that just underlined his frustration and concern.

'She has a calendar at home. This month's slogan is, "Good morning. Let the stress begin." I think that about sums it up.'

Annie shook her head slowly. 'She'd be lost without you. She's lucky to have you.'

'No, I'm lucky to have her, lucky to have had both of them. That's why I'm here, because I can be, and because I love them more than I can say. My parents are crap at this sort of thing, my brother's life is already chaos. It's me or nobody. And it's fine, you know? He did a lot for me when I was a kid. They both did. I'm happy to do it.'

Happy? He didn't look happy. He looked saddened and hunted. Because the threat was hanging over him?

His choice. His business. Just because she wouldn't be able to cope with such a massive question mark in her life, it didn't mean he couldn't.

And she was supposed to be keeping it impersonal and professional and detached! She closed the lid on the conversation and looked at the whiteboard.

'So what's what here today?'

'Not a lot. It's been the usual Friday night, I gather, but it had all calmed down by the time I got here and now it's quiet. There are a few in cubicles who need a look. Want to give me a hand?'

'That's what I'm here for,' she said with a bright, professional smile, and with another glance at the whiteboard she reached for the next set of notes.

It picked up, of course, with a vengeance.

They didn't get time for coffee, and it was almost two before they found time for lunch.

'Right,' he said firmly, taking her by the arm and steering her towards the door. 'It's quiet for a moment. It won't last, the sporting injuries will be pouring in in a minute, so we're going for lunch. Now.'

She hung back, thinking of that detachment that was flying out of the window again. 'I need to tell them to page me—'

'They will. They know. They sent me to get you and feed you. Apparently you get crabby when your blood sugar's low.'

She removed her arm from his grip but kept walking. She could talk and argue, and she was seriously starving. 'Who said I get crabby?'

'Kate.'

'Hmph. She can talk. She's vile if she doesn't get chocolate.'

'I'll take her back a bar as a peace offering,' he said with a grin. 'In fact, I'll get several so I've got some in stock. Anything for a quiet life.'

They grabbed two filled rolls, the only things left, he picked up a handful of chocolate bars, true to his word, and they collected their coffee and headed back outside.

Annie turned her face up to the sun and sighed with contentment. 'I can't believe this weather.'

'Gorgeous, isn't it? Oh, that reminds me. I've got a beach-hut key for you. Marnie thought it was a great idea. She *really* likes you, by the way.'

There was something in his tone of voice that made her laugh. 'Oh, dear. Is she giving you grief?'

'A bit. Time I settled down, et cetera, et cetera. And she thinks she knows your mother from book club years ago. Or, at least, she knew a Joanna Brooks, who you reminded her of, and Chloe was chattering about MamaJo coming down to the beach, so I assumed it could be her?'

'Yes, it could well be. Mum lived here for years before she came down to London to help me with the girls, and she was involved with all kinds of things, and she still goes to the book club. I'll ask her if she knows Marnie.'

'They'll get together,' he warned, and she laughed.

'That would be a nightmare—can you imagine the conversation? The girls didn't stop talking to her about you yesterday afternoon and Mum was hanging on every word. Grace thought you were lovely, by the way.'

'I am lovely,' he said, deadpan, but his eyes were laughing.

He was, but she absolutely wasn't going there. Instead she laughed, pinched one of the chocolate bars from his little stash and peeled it open.

'Hey, they were for Kate!'

'Oh, come on, not even Kate's that crabby—unless you've upset her again?'

He gave a soft chuckle. 'No. Not since I told her to back off, but she was really mean about you.'

'She's harmless. *You* were mean.'

'She was deeply nosy. And she keeps giving us looks.'

Annie rolled her eyes. 'Because we keep going off for lunch and coffee together!'

'True, but that's only because we grab the quiet times so there aren't many options. So—when are you free again, talking of going off together?'

She shrugged, wishing it could be tonight,

knowing it was a bad idea. All of it. And her self-discipline was failing miserably. Time to shore it up.

'I don't know. I'll ask Mum, but she's a bit too curious about you at the moment. I don't want to encourage her.' There. Nicely detached.

'Next Friday?'

Or not, she thought as she felt a wave of disappointment. 'No, I can't do Friday. We're away for the weekend. It's my uncle's sixtieth birthday and he's having a big family party and we're taking my grandmother.'

He frowned thoughtfully. 'Of course, if she could look after the children, you could help me move the little playhouse one evening. That shouldn't raise too many red flags for her and I'm sure we could drag it out for a couple of hours. Tomorrow, perhaps?'

One eyebrow gave a suggestive little wiggle, and her resolve was instantly demolished by the teasing promise in his eyes.

'I'm sure we could. It's a good enough excuse. I'll ask her.'

'Do that,' he said, and winking at her as he

gathered up all their wrappers and stood up. 'I might even take you out for dinner afterwards.'

Dinner? That sounded more and more like a date, she thought, and felt the tingle of anticipation all the way down to her toes.

So much for detachment and self-discipline.

'You won't believe what I've won! Dinner for two at that lovely new restaurant on the seafront!' Her mother beamed and waved the voucher at her.

'How? Where? You never win anything!'

'Well, I did this time. We went to the church fete and I bought some raffle tickets and my number came up. I'll pin it on the board before I lose it, although goodness knows who I'd go with. Maybe we can get someone else to babysit and we can go together. So, how was work?'

'Busy, and I'm on again tomorrow and it'll be just as bad if not worse. Were the girls good for you?'

'Absolutely fine. They're always good.'

'Not always,' she said with a laugh. She could see them in the garden now, squabbling over something in the sandpit, and she knew it was just a matter of time before it all kicked off.

'Can I ask you another favour? Ed's grandparents have got a playhouse they don't need any more, and they've said we can have it, and I know the girls will love it. Are you OK to have it in the garden? I don't want to presume—'

'Don't be silly! That would be lovely, and they'll get huge fun out of it. Of course it's all right. Where were you going to put it?'

She shrugged. 'I don't know, it's your garden, Mum. I imagine it needs a firm, flat base. I don't even know how big it is.'

'How about the corner of the patio? You know, that narrow bit at the side. I can't imagine it would be too big for that.'

They went out into the garden where the girls were playing nicely now in their little sandpit, their squabble evidently over.

'Hello, Mummy! Look, we made a duck pond!'

She admired it for a moment, then looked round the garden and felt a wave of guilt. It was such a lovely little garden, but it wasn't huge and the girls were gradually taking it over with all their toys and games and multi-coloured clutter.

Far from minding, though, her mother was eyeing up the corner of the patio and smiling. 'This would be fine. We never sit here because it's too narrow, so it's not doing anything useful and it'll be nice and handy to keep an eye on them. How are you going to get it here?'

'He's got a trailer, apparently—he suggested tomorrow evening. Could you keep an eye on the girls while we do it? I'll have to help him, he can't do it on his own and his grandmother can't help him— Oh, that reminds me, she thinks she knows you. Marnie Shackleton? She used to belong to a book group.'

'Marnie? Marnie's his grandmother? Oh, how is she?' her mother asked fondly. 'Such a nice woman—she stopped coming, her husband was ill and she couldn't leave him alone any longer. I did miss her, she was lovely. And he's still alive?'

'Oh, yes, he's alive, but he's not at all well, though. That's why Ed's home.'

A little frown pleated her brow. 'Oh, of course,

you said. So sad. Well, certainly I'll babysit tomorrow so you can do that, and you must give her my love and tell her we'll get together some time. Maybe I can go and have a coffee with her one day. So what do they want for the playhouse?'

'Nothing. They just want it out of the way, I think. Oh, and Ed's lent us a key for their beach hut so we can take the girls down there when they're not using it.'

'Oh, how kind! Well, we really must give them something,' she said, and then her eyes lit up. 'Oh, I've got an idea, why don't you use the restaurant voucher and take Ed out to dinner? After all, he's the one who's going to have to move it.'

Oh, the guilt, after what they'd planned! And she couldn't let her mother give away her voucher, but then she had a brilliant idea.

'No, Mum, you won it, you should go. Maybe Ed could look after his grandfather one evening and you and Marnie could go out? After all, it's her we should be thanking, not Ed. I'm sure she'd love it, and so would you, and you could get to know her again.'

Which was in *no* way a good idea, she thought belatedly, but Marnie must be so lonely and isolated, and Annie was sure she could do with all the friends she could get. Caring for a terminally ill relative was physically and emotionally draining and the break would do Marnie good. And so what if the two of them did a little matchmaking? It couldn't do any harm, so long as they weren't both overly disappointed when it all came to nothing.

Which it would, she reminded herself firmly, and crushed her own sense of disappointment.

'Oh, it looks lovely there,' Jo said, beaming. 'It's just perfect!'

Ed gave a soft laugh. 'Well, I don't know about perfect. I oiled the door hinges and gave it a bit of a sweep but it could do with a thorough clean. It's years since it's been used.'

'I'm sure we can manage that. Thank you so much, the girls will get so much pleasure from it,' Annie said. She looked on the verge of tears, and the girls were jumping up and down in excitement and couldn't wait to get inside.

'Go on, then, open the door and go in,' she said to them.

'Me first!'

'No, I'm the oldest!'

'Hold hands and go in together, and play nicely or I'll ask Ed to take it back again,' she said firmly, and in they went like lambs.

He stifled a laugh and turned to her mother. 'Marnie sends her love, by the way. She'd like to see you again.'

'Well, that's lovely because I want to see her, too, and I'd like to thank her for the playhouse and the offer of the use of the beach hut, but this involves you, I'm afraid, yet again. I won a voucher for a meal for two and I thought I could take her, if she'd like that, but I gather she can't leave her husband alone—'

'What a lovely idea! Thank you. I'm sure she'd be over the moon, she hasn't been out in the evening for ages. And of course I'll sit with him. It's not a problem. I'll liaise with Annie and find a time when we're all free.' He glanced at Annie, and then back to her mother.

'In fact, talking of favours, are you busy now?

I thought, since it's a nice evening, I might take Annie down to the beach hut and show her where everything is and how it works. Things like turning the gas on and so forth, and then you could maybe take the girls down there tomorrow.'

'Oh, what a marvellous idea! But she hasn't eaten yet.'

He gave what he hoped was an innocent smile. 'That's fine. We can get fish and chips and make a cup of tea in the hut.'

'Oh, that sounds like a great idea. Go now, while it's still nice. I'll get the girls to bed when they've had a bit of a play.'

'Excuse me? I am here,' Annie interrupted, hands on hips and eyebrows raised. 'I need to shower and change before I can go anywhere.'

Ed met her eyes and managed not to laugh. She had a smear of green on one cheek from the outside of the playhouse, and he was sure he didn't look any better. He rammed his hands in his pockets to stop him from reaching out and wiping the little green streak away with his fingers. 'Me, too. I'll come back and pick you up in half an hour.'

* * *

Annie crumpled up the paper and wiped her mouth on the back of her hand. 'That was amazing. I haven't had fish and chips out of the paper for years and I don't remember it ever being so good.'

'Ah, well, you have to know where to go. Sometimes it's gruesome.' He took the ball of paper from her, walked over to a bin on the prom and put the rubbish in, and then leant on the rail at the edge and smiled contentedly. 'Just listen to that.'

She went and stood beside him, staring out over the sea, listening to the gentle slap of the waves against the breakwater, the keening of the gulls wheeling overhead, the distant putter of an outboard motor.

Peace.

He shifted, turning to face her, his hip propped on the railings, and his eyes searched her face.

'You OK?'

'Mmm. Just thinking how lovely it is here. The girls are going to love it. It's so kind of you to lend it to us, and the playhouse—well, that's just amazing. There's no way I could have afforded it. We just don't have the resources, not until I've finished clearing up the financial mess left by my ex and my maternity leave, and they'll have hours of fun in it…'

She felt herself well up again, and shook her head.

'Hey.' He tipped her chin up and smiled at her. 'None of that. It's only an old toy we didn't need.'

'No. It's much more than that. It's not the gift, although that's amazing, it's the way you've given it, given your time as much as anything. I couldn't have moved it by myself even if we'd bought it second-hand from someone else, and I didn't know about it, you need never have mentioned it, but you did, because you're kind and thoughtful and generous—' She broke off because she simply couldn't speak any more, and she felt his fingers stroke her cheek, brushing away the tears.

'I'm not your ex, Annie,' he reminded her gently, and she looked up and met his intent gaze.

'You don't have to tell me that. Believe me, I

know.' She did. Oh, how well she knew it. They couldn't be more different. She could trust Ed. With her heart? With the hearts of her children?

Yes. Absolutely, and he'd never let them down. But she couldn't let it get that far, because he might die, and then they'd lose him…

She squeezed her eyes shut and sucked in a breath against the stab of pain, and she felt his hands slip to her shoulders, curling round them as he drew her towards him.

'Ah, Annie, come here.'

His arms closed around her, easing her up against his chest, and she leant her head on it and listened to the steady, even beat of his heart beneath her ear. So calming. So reassuring.

I love you. Please don't die.

He pressed his lips to her hair. 'I brought some Prosecco,' he murmured. 'Do you want it here, or back at my house?'

She sucked in a breath and tilted her head back so she could read his eyes. Fire smouldered in them, carefully banked but there nonetheless. She put her fears on hold and gave herself to the moment. *Carpe diem…*

'Here, I think.' And then she added, 'Are we still talking about the Prosecco?' and he smiled slowly.

'Well, Dr Brooks, you read my mind.'

She smiled back, turned with him and went into the beach hut, her heart tripping. He closed the doors, leaving a chink of light through the top of the curtains, and reached for her.

'Oh, what a lovely beach hut! It's so pretty!'

'It is, isn't it?'

And it was a miracle all the pretty pale blue paint hadn't blistered off the walls.

Annie turned away from her mother, stuck her bottom lip out and blew her breath up over her face to cool it. That padded bench seat her mother was perched on now had a whole set of X-rated memories attached to it, and her face was going to be a total giveaway.

'Oh, look, Mum. The girls are having fun on the sand already. They just love it. This is going to be such a blessing.'

'I'm sure it will. Immensely civilised. Do you

know how to put the kettle on? We could have coffee. I brought all the makings.'

'Sure.'

If she could remember. He had shown her, but only after he'd addled her brains with that sexy smile and those clever little manoeuvres—

Don't think about it!

But just to remind her, the empty Prosecco bottle was standing there on the side, too. They'd meant to take the bottle away with them, but they'd forgotten. She'd better mention it before her mother did.

'So did you get fish and chips?' her mother was asking.

'Yes. We got it from the kiosk down on the prom on our way here, and it was really delicious. We just sat here with the gulls wheeling overhead and ate it out of the paper and had a glass of wine. It was lovely down here, so peaceful, and we hardly saw a soul.'

'I looked into getting a beach hut, you know, but they're so expensive, even to hire for a week. Our weather's just not reliable enough.'

And now they were talking about the weather.

Well, it was safer than dwelling any longer on what she and Ed Shackleton had done here last night with only the gulls for company…

He missed her.

Marnie and Jo had gone out for dinner, and he was sitting in the garden of his grandparents' house and watching his grandfather sleeping through the patio door. The nightlight was on, bathing the old man in a soft, golden glow.

He looked utterly peaceful and at ease, and there was nothing to do, so he rang Annie.

'Hi.'

'Hi—is everything all right?'

He gave a quiet and slightly despairing laugh. 'Yeah, I suppose so. He's in bed, and I'm just sitting in the garden, watching him sleep through the window.'

'How is he?'

'Not great. He's peaceful enough now, but he's going downhill fast and I don't think it'll be long.' His voice sounded rough, and he cleared his throat. 'Sorry, didn't mean to unload like that.'

'It's fine, don't apologise. I'm so sorry.'

'Don't be. I want it over, Annie, for all our sakes. I just can't bear watching him—'

'It must be so hard.'

Her voice was gentle, reaching out to him, and he closed his eyes tightly against the stinging.

'Tell me what you're doing. Tell me about the girls. Just—talk to me, Annie…'

So she did, and he sat there with his eyes closed and listened to the warmth of her voice as she talked about the children and what they'd been doing, and the fun they'd had in the playhouse.

'We cleaned it out on Monday after we got back from the beach, and I found an old dress covered in tiny flowers and cut it up to make curtains, and we put their toy kitchen in it and they cooked supper for us. I really can't thank you enough. And Mum was so ridiculously pleased that Marnie wanted to go out with her tonight. I hope they're having a nice time. They both deserve it.'

'I've heard it's really good,' he said, finding his voice again. 'Maybe we should go one day.'

'That would be lovely.'

Except they weren't supposed to be going public with this, but frankly he didn't care any more what anyone thought, not for himself, although when he left Yoxburgh he didn't want her hurt by the damage to her reputation.

He frowned. He didn't want to think about leaving, for a whole host of reasons, but suddenly Annie seemed to be at the top of the list.

He glanced back at the house, just as the sitting-room light came on.

'Ah. Marnie's back. I'll talk to you soon.'

'OK. You take care.'

'You, too. Sleep well.'

He hung up, got to his feet and walked quietly back to the house. He found Marnie in the kitchen, putting the kettle on.

'Hi. How was it?'

'Oh, lovely! It was so nice to see her again—she's a lovely woman, I'd forgotten just how nice she is. And she thinks you're fabulous, by the way.'

He gave a wry smile. 'Does she, now?'

'Yes, she does, and I don't think she's alone.' Her smile faded and she searched his eyes.

'Don't hurt her, Edward. I know you don't mean to, but as long as you're still running from this thing, anyone that gets in the way is in danger of getting trampled.'

'I won't hurt her. She's not looking for permanence, Marnie. We're just having a bit of adult fun.'

She arched a slender brow at him in the way she had when he'd lied to her as a toddler, and he closed his eyes. 'Oh, come on, Marnie, we're all adults. I'm allowed a sex life.'

'Of course you are, darling. You're also allowed to be happy.'

He swallowed hard. 'I am happy.'

'Are you? I don't think so. I think you'd like to be, and I think Annie's got the ability to make you very happy, but I'm very afraid you won't let it happen.'

He turned away, not prepared to discuss this with her, or anyone else, for that matter. Not even himself.

'Grumps is settled now. His breathing's a bit rough. I think he might have a chest infection.'

'Antibiotics?'

It wasn't a simple question, and it didn't have a simple answer. He turned back, propping himself against the edge of the kitchen counter.

'I don't know. What do you think?'

Marnie shrugged her shoulders. They were getting thinner with the strain and worry. 'I don't know either. Will you stay the night? Keep an eye on him?'

'Of course I will. I'm not working tomorrow.'

He hugged her, feeling how frail she was getting, how drained by it all. 'I'm glad you had a nice time with Jo.'

'So am I. Oh, Ed, what will I do without you?' she said in a small voice that broke his heart.

'You aren't without me.'

'Not now, I'm not, but we all know you're not staying.' She eased away from him and turned back to the kettle, made two mugs of tea and handed him one. 'Here. Come and sit down and let me tell you all about the food. It was amazing.'

There was drama at work the next morning.

James was supposed to be working, but there

was no sign of him, and at nine he stuck his head in and told them that his wife Connie was in labour.

'Sorry, guys, got to bail on you, and I'm supposed to be on over the weekend, too. I don't suppose there's any way you could cover me, Andy, could you?'

Andy sighed sharply and shook his head. 'Oh, James, I would, but it's Daniel's birthday and we're having a family day out to the zoo. I can do Sunday—Annie, any chance you could do tomorrow?'

'No, she can't, you're away, aren't you?' James said.

She shrugged. 'I'm meant to be. It's my uncle's sixtieth and my mother and grandmother are going as well. To be honest, I'm not bothered, but it relies on my mother being prepared to take the girls away on her own.' She flapped a hand at him. 'I'll ask her. I'm sure it'll be fine. James, leave it with us. Connie needs you, and this is your first baby. You go back to your wife and forget about us. We'll sort it.'

'Sure?'

'Sure. Go.'

He hugged her, slapped Andy on the back and ran.

'OK. So how are we going to sort it?' Andy asked, propping himself up against the wall and smiling at her wryly. 'Got a locum up your sleeve?'

Annie rolled her eyes and laughed. 'No, I've got a mother who's a saint. It's fine. I'll spend the rest of the weekend cleaning the house from end to end and weeding the garden to make up for it. You do Sunday, and I'll do tomorrow. Deal?'

'Deal. Right, go and get coffee and ring your mother while it's quiet. I'll cover.'

'Don't forget to tell Lucy.'

'I won't. Shoo.'

She shooed, and on the way to the café she called her mother. The response was predictable.

'Oh, how exciting! Well, it's a pity you can't come, of course, but they won't have a baby every weekend so of course I can do it. I'll let Mike and Sally know. Are you planning on coming up on Saturday after work?'

'I don't know. It hardly seems worth it, really.

I won't get there till nearly nine, and then you'll be coming back after breakfast. If you're OK, I'll leave it. I thought I'd blitz the house.'

'Oh, darling! That seems a bit unfair.'

'What, more unfair than me dumping the kids on you yet again so I can work? Hardly. Look, I've got to fly, I've only got a few minutes and I need to grab a coffee. I'll see you later.'

She hung up, ordered her coffee, which immediately made her think of Ed, and then thought of nothing else.

If she was home alone tonight and Saturday night, maybe she could see him. Stay over, even.

Heart pounding in anticipation, she sent him a text, and seconds later her phone rang.

'How about tonight?'

CHAPTER EIGHT

SHE WENT STRAIGHT into his arms.

He was waiting for her in the garden and came through the arch to greet her, and he looked awful.

'What's happened?'

'Nothing,' he said into her hair. 'I'm tired, that's all. Rough day. God, I've missed you.'

She lifted her head and his lips found hers unerringly. 'Come to bed,' he said against her mouth, and she nodded. She wasn't sure what was going on, but he needed her, and that was all she needed to know.

He made love to her with an intensity that stunned her. It was as if he was trying to lose himself, to escape from reality into a world where nothing existed except the two of them, and he held back nothing.

He didn't need to. She was with him all the

way, clinging to him, fighting whatever hidden demons he was trying to exorcise, and when it was over he rolled onto his back, taking her with him, and held her tight against him as the sawing of his breath eased and their hearts slowed with the receding shock waves.

She let him lie there for a while, but she could still hear the cogs turning, the emotion churning through him, and she tilted her head to study him.

His face was expressionless. She lifted a hand and cradled his jaw, feeling the stubble rasp against her palm.

'Are you OK?'

He turned his head towards her, his smile crooked. It didn't reach his eyes. 'Yeah. Sorry. I've just had a really rough day with my grandfather. I'm not very good company, I'm afraid.'

'It's fine, don't worry about it. What's wrong with him?'

She felt his whole body tense, as if he was bracing himself to talk about it. 'His chest is a bit congested.'

His voice was soft and a little raw, and she

could hear his heart pounding under her ear. She moved so she could see him better. 'Pneumonia?'

'Yeah, and he's got two advance directives with a whole bunch of conditions. No hospital, no resuscitation, no unnecessary intervention. The GP's been great—it's Andy's wife, Lucy Gallagher. She only works part time, but she's come out even when she's been off duty, and she came out yesterday morning after she dropped the children off. She wasn't supposed to be working, but she'd been worried about him the day before. And we had a long talk.'

'And?'

He shrugged again. There was a hopelessness about the gesture that tugged at her heartstrings, and she wrapped her arms around him and hugged him. 'He's dying, Annie. It's just a matter of time now, and maybe not much of that.'

'Do you need to be there?'

'No. Marnie sent me home. She wanted to be alone with him. And there's nothing I can do.'

There was nothing to say to that, no platitude she could offer. Only herself. She cradled his cheek again, turning his face towards her so she could feather a gentle kiss on his lips.

'I love you.'

He stiffened and closed his eyes, but he didn't pull away. 'Annie, no,' he pleaded, his voice cracking. 'Don't do this. Don't go there—'

'I am there. I didn't mean to be, but I am. There are no implications for you, Ed. I'm not asking anything of you, I'm just telling you I love you, and that I'm here for you, whenever you need me, whatever you need from me—a shoulder, a way to lose yourself from reality, a sounding board, whatever.'

He let out his breath on a long, shuddering sigh and pulled her closer. 'Just hold me,' he said roughly, and she did.

She held him all night, in one way or another, spooning around him when he turned away, holding him close after he woke in the night and made love to her again with a desperation that made her weep silently for him.

And then, at five o'clock, the phone rang.

She couldn't get hold of him.

She'd contacted James and told him that Ed

wouldn't be coming in, and because Connie's baby had been born after midnight, she was still in hospital so he'd come in to help out for a few hours.

'You didn't need to come in,' she tutted, but he just smiled the smile of a man who'd thought he'd never be a father and hugged her.

'Yes, I did, and it's fine. I'll do a few hours, that's all. I've already been and had a cuddle with him.'

'Got a name yet?'

His smile was a little off kilter. 'Joseph. There was no contest.'

Of course. After Connie's first husband, Joe. He'd been James's best friend, and he was the reason they were together. She smiled back at him and squeezed his hand. 'That's lovely. A good, strong name.'

'We thought so. So what's happening with Ed's grandfather?'

'He's got pneumonia. Ed didn't think it would be long.'

'Ah. I'd better factor him out of the equation for a bit, then. I wonder if you and Andy could do a few more shifts? It's going to be really tight and I don't want to bail on Connie. Can we share the load?'

'Of course we can. I'm sure Mum won't mind under the circumstances. She knows his grandmother.'

'Good. Right, better crack on and clear what we can before I go off.'

They set to work, and every time she had a moment she checked her phone, but there was nothing from him. She didn't want to pester him. She'd sent a text saying she was thinking of them all and would he let her know how things were, and she was sure he'd come back to her at some point with an update.

James went off to collect his wife and son and take them home, and she battled through the afternoon with the help of the registrar and a reasonably competent F2. And they managed, but her mind wasn't entirely on the job and she was glad nothing major cropped up.

She handed over at six, after finishing off the paperwork on a nasty sports injury she'd admitted, and still there was nothing from him, so she went home, showered and changed into linen trousers and a loose linen mix shirt and went to see if she could find him.

He wasn't at home, and she drove past his grandparents' house and saw his car on the drive with several others. His parents and brother? Very likely. About time they showed up, she thought grimly, but actually he'd seemed happy enough to shoulder the burden with Marnie without their help, and it had probably been better for Ned. Calmer, more continuity.

She wondered what was happening.

Nothing she was a part of or could help with, she was sure, so she drove home, rang the girls and spoke to them and her mother, wished her uncle a happy birthday, heard all about the party she'd missed and then hung up again.

She cooked herself something to eat, but she had no appetite and there was nothing on the television and the book she was reading didn't hold her attention at all.

She was at a loss, unable to settle, so she drove to the cliff-top car park and pulled up close to the steps. The cars were still there on the drive, nobody coming or going, and she could almost feel the suspense hanging over the house.

She couldn't do this. Couldn't sit and watch and wait for something to happen. It seemed too intrusive, almost stalker-like, but she couldn't bear to be too far away, so she locked the car and walked down the steps to the deserted beach. She had a signal on her phone, the key of the beach hut in her pocket. She could sit in there and wait for news.

Except the doors were open.

Her footsteps slowed to a halt. Should she walk past, see if it was someone she recognised? If not, it wouldn't matter, the beach wasn't private.

And if it was Marnie?

She heard the murmur of a voice, but it was too far away to hear who it was or what they were saying. And then, a moment later, her phone beeped.

He felt numb.

They'd been waiting for this for so long, and

yet in the end it had seemed sudden, and he hadn't been ready for it.

Were you ever ready? Probably not.

They'd all been together, his father falling apart as the reality finally penetrated, he and his brother stony-faced and fighting back tears, and Marnie, quiet, calm, holding his hand and talking softly to him as the old man had gently slipped away.

After the battle of the past forty-eight hours, the silence had seemed like a blessing, but it was as if no one had quite known what to do at that point so he'd stepped in, the doctor in him taking over as he'd picked up his stethoscope and listened for his grandfather's heart.

'He's gone,' he said softly, and turned off the oxygen, squeezed Marnie's shoulder and walked out into the garden. The patio doors had been open, the rest of them gathered in the shade, waiting for news, and they saw his face and started to cry.

It was all too much for him.

He went back in the other way, picked up the

key of the beach hut and left the house. The doctor would come later, then the undertaker, all the wheels grinding into motion, but that would keep. For now, he just wanted silence.

And Annie.

He opened the hut, sat down on the bench seat where they'd made love just days ago, and stared blankly at the sea. He was sure the feeling would return at some point, but for now he felt nothing, just a curious emptiness where his heart used to be.

His phone rang, jiggling in his pocket, still on silent. His brother. He answered it reluctantly. 'Hi, there.'

'Where are you, Ed?'

'I just needed some air. I won't be long.'

'Are you all right?'

Was he? 'Yeah, I'm fine, Pete,' he lied. 'I'll see you soon.'

Then he sent a text to Annie.

He's gone.

The reply pinged back instantly.

So sorry. Where are you?

At the beach hut. Where are you?

He heard footsteps, and she appeared in the doorway, and the hole where his heart had been was suddenly filled again.

'I'm here,' she said, and he stood up and wrapped his arms around her and hung on for dear life.

The next week was filled with admin.

He decided to let his family take over and carry that part of the load, and on Tuesday he went back to work.

Andy was the first person he saw.

'Hey. How are you?'

'I'll do. Andy, will you thank Lucy, please? She's been amazing—'

He broke off, his voice cracking, and he cleared his throat. 'Um—I need to be busy. What can I do?'

'I'm going to put you on Minors. The cubicles

are stacked to the rafters for some reason, and it'll keep you occupied for hours.'

Minors? He wanted something good and gory, something to challenge him, to get his teeth into, but he realised he probably wasn't up to it. He nodded. 'Thanks. Right, well, I'll go and get on.'

He had to deal with all the others, of course, coming up to him and offering condolences, but he just thanked them and carried on working, and bit by bit he started to feel a little more normal.

Until Annie came out of Resus and saw him.

'Hey, what are you doing here?' she asked, her voice soft with concern.

'I need to work.'

To his surprise she didn't argue, just nodded. 'OK. Want a coffee?'

'Not really. If you're going over, can you get me one?'

'Sure.'

He watched her go, aching to go with her, knowing it was a bad idea. Ever since she'd told him she loved him on Friday night, he'd known he had to back off. Not that he wanted to. Left to his own devices, he'd keep her with him all day and all night, but it wasn't fair.

There was no way he was going to let her face what he'd had to face, the decisions he'd had to make for his grandfather, the endless agony of watching him die inch by inch.

If it came to it, he wanted a stranger making those decisions, someone who wouldn't be torn apart as Marnie had been torn apart and ground down by the unrelenting advance of the disease.

So when she came back, he thanked her for the coffee and carried on working. He even offered to pay for it, which earned him a stern look as she turned and walked away.

Damn.

'Mum, I hate to ask you but are you busy to-night?'

'No, darling. Why? Do you want to go and see Ed?'

'Please. He's back at work, and he looks awful. Blank. Empty. I'm worried about him.'

'And I'm worried about you. Marnie told me

when we went out for dinner that he hasn't had the test.'

Wow. The two women really had got straight down to business. 'He has,' she corrected. 'He just hasn't got the result—and he's never told Marnie that, so please don't.'

'Of course I won't. But it doesn't stop me worrying about you.'

'There's no need, really. I'm a grown woman, I know the score.'

'It doesn't stop you hurting.'

Annie smiled gently. 'I know that.'

She kissed her mother's cheek, let herself out and walked round to his house. There was no answer to the front doorbell, so she walked round to the back and went up on tiptoe and peered over the gate.

His car was there, and she could hear the steady, rhythmic creak of the swing seat. The gate yielded to her touch, and she went in, ducked under the arch and met his eyes.

'You didn't answer the doorbell.'

'I didn't hear it.'

'May I come in?'

He shrugged. 'Looks like you have.'

She sighed softly and sat down at the other end of the seat, breaking his rhythm. He set it going again, steadfastly ignoring her.

Fair enough. She hadn't expected it to be easy.

'Have you eaten?'

He shook his head. 'I'm not hungry.'

'I thought you'd say that. You haven't eaten all day, and nor have I. Let's go and get fish and chips.'

The swing seat stopped for a moment, then started again, the creak beginning to get on her nerves.

'Why are you doing this?'

'Because someone has to, and it strikes me there's nobody else. Who's looking after Marnie?'

'My parents. She's staying with them. I'm not sure how long it'll last.'

She nodded. Going back to the house would be hard for her. Easier, maybe, if she hadn't gone away. And when she came back, Ed would be with her, she was sure of it. But for now…

'So while she's away, you can neglect yourself?'

He got to his feet, angry now. 'OK, have it your own way,' he growled. 'We'll go and get fish and chips.'

Well, at least she'd got a reaction out of him. She waited while he snagged a jumper in case it got colder, locked the house, opened the gates and started the car.

'Well, get in, then.'

She got in, and he drove out, shut the gates, put down the roof of the car and headed for the chip shop. He didn't ask her what she wanted, just went in and left her there with the keys in the ignition. She wasn't stupid enough to leave the car, and a few minutes later he came back with a plain paper parcel and handed it to her.

'Cod and chips twice, with salt and vinegar. That do you?'

'Yes, it'll do me fine. Thank you.'

He made a sound somewhere between a laugh and a snort, and headed to the cliff-top, parking in Marnie's drive.

'We'll go to the beach hut,' he said, and set off without her, leaving her to follow meekly behind.

Or not so meekly.

She knew what he was doing. He was trying to drive her out, but she could handle that. He was hurting. She could see it in every line of his body, every glance of his eyes, every word he spoke to her.

Because he loved her, too?

Very likely. Well, he'd be going soon, and there'd be plenty of time to deal with the fallout then. In the meantime, she hurried after him, trying to keep up with his punishing stride.

And then she stopped hurrying, followed him at her own pace and arrived at the beach hut just in time for him to have opened it all up and got out the chairs.

'Want plates?'

She raised a brow, handed him one of the packets and settled back to eat.

He watched her out of the corner of his eye.

God, he wanted her. Wanted to hold her close, bury himself in her and lose himself. But first, he realised, he wanted to eat. He was ravenous, and he ate every morsel.

And then, with a hint of a smile in her eyes, she handed him the remains of her chips and watched him finish them.

'Better?'

And at last he smiled. It was a pretty poor effort, but she was massively relieved to see it, and she leant over and kissed him. 'Hello again.'

His smile became wry. 'Sorry. I've been a bastard.'

'No, you've been hurting. It's fine. Just don't shut me out, please? You don't have to put on an act for me, Ed.'

He gave a soft laugh. 'Do you know what I really want to do? I want to take you to bed.'

'So what's stopping you?'

'Proximity.'

'What, the lack of it?'

'No, of the house. There are things I have to do before Marnie comes home. Get the loaned hospital bed returned. Reinstate the dining room. Give the house a thorough clean.'

'Let me help you.'

He stared at her. 'You'd do that?'

Annie rolled her eyes. 'Of course I'd do that!

What, you think I just want the good bits? Sex and Prosecco? It sounds like the title of a really tacky book.'

He laughed softly, then searched her eyes intently.

'Are you serious?'

'Of course I'm serious. Shall we go and have a look now?'

'Really?'

'Really. Come on. Have you got the keys?'

'Of course.'

They shut up the beach hut and made their way back up the steps to the empty, silent house. It was the first time she'd been in, only the second time she'd been there, the first being when they'd collected the playhouse for the children, and for all it had weary décor and dated furnishings, she loved it.

'Wow, what a fabulous house.'

'It is. It's simple, but it doesn't need to be fancy. It's got the sea view.'

She turned and looked out through the sitting-room window, and shook her head slowly. 'That is so beautiful.'

'It's better from the bedrooms. You can see up to Aldeburgh and down to Felixstowe.'

He stopped talking, glanced towards the door, and she slipped her hand into his. 'Right, let's have a look at this room, then.'

He nodded briefly, led her back down the hall and opened a door on the other side, near the back.

She heard the slight suck of his breath, and squeezed his hand before letting go. 'OK. Let's get started.'

They worked to midnight, then went back to his house and went to bed.

She didn't mean to stay, but somehow they ended up falling asleep, and his alarm woke them at six.

'Yikes!' she squealed, and catapulted out of bed and tugged on her clothes. 'I'll see you at work—are you OK?'

He smiled wryly. 'I'm fine. Thank you, Annie. Go on, go and sort the kids out. I'll see you later.'

To his surprise, he *was* fine. She'd helped him overcome the first hurdle with the house, tackled the thing he'd been dreading most and driven out the ghosts. And fed him. He mustn't forget that. He hadn't realised how hungry he'd been until she'd made him eat last night.

He stretched, threw back the covers and headed for the shower.

The funeral was lovely, a celebration of Ned's life, and both Marnie and Ed stood up to talk about him.

How did they do that? Annie had no idea, but they did, and it was incredibly moving and touching and funny. They went back to the house afterwards, restored to normal after a lot of hard work and effort, and everyone mingled in the garden.

Her mother found someone else she knew, and while they were engaged in conversation Marnie sought her out.

'Annie.'

'Oh, Marnie. How are you?'

She steered her away and walked slowly down the garden with her. 'I'm fine. I'm sad, but I'm fine. I was so lucky to have him, and for all the agony of the past few years, I wouldn't change a moment of it—well, apart from taking away his suffering, but I couldn't do that, sadly.' She stopped walking and took Annie's hand and held it tight.

'I wanted to thank you so much for everything you've done to help Ed in the past week. He tells me you've been amazing.'

'Oh, Marnie, it was nothing. I couldn't let him face it alone, or you. A problem shared and all that, and it really wasn't so much once we got down to it.'

She nodded. 'He loves you, you know.'

'I know. I love him, too, and I've told him that.'

She laughed softly. 'I don't suppose he wanted to hear it?'

'No.'

'No, he wouldn't. And he won't do anything about it, because he's afraid he might have the defective gene and he won't find out. He's told me he has, of course, but I know he's lying. He's never been able to lie to me, not since he was a toddler and stole some sweets from a jar. He still gets that same shifty look.'

That made Annie laugh. 'I can imagine. He

has had the test, you know,' she went on, and Marnie smiled sadly.

'I know. I also know he hasn't had the result. Just call it intuition. And I need to know he's going to be all right. I'm just so afraid for him, so racked with guilt because it came from me, but thank God my daughter hasn't got it, and my son won't suffer from it. And of course Ed's brother, Peter, hasn't got the gene either, but I just don't know about Ed and I need to know, Annie. I need to know so I can die in peace.'

Oh, no.

'Marnie, I can't ask him to get the result,' she said gently. 'It has to be his decision.'

She nodded. 'I know. I'm just being selfish. But don't let him drive you away, Annie. He'd try to, because he's got some crazy notion that if he doesn't let himself love, then he won't be missing out, but you and I both know that's nonsense and he's got so much to give.'

Annie glanced up, catching his eye across the lawn, and smiled. 'He has. Don't worry, Marnie, I'm working on it. And I'm not a quitter.'

'I'm glad to hear it, because even if he has

the gene, even if he'll never have children of his own, he'd be a wonderful father to your girls.'

'I know. I just have to convince him of that.'

'Well, good luck with that one. He's nothing if not stubborn. He's so like Ned in that respect.' She kissed Annie's cheek. 'I have to go and circulate. I just wanted to thank you.'

'My pleasure.'

Marnie walked away, quickly absorbed by the throng, and Ed appeared at her side. 'Don't tell me. She wants you to get me to get the result.'

'Actually, she wanted to thank me for helping you,' she corrected, only partially honestly, but she wasn't dumping Marnie in it. 'That was a lovely service. He would have been proud of you.'

He gave a huff of laughter and glanced around. 'How long do you think I need to stay?'

'To the end. Marnie needs you. The next few hours will be the hardest for her. Don't leave her alone.'

She went up on tiptoe and kissed his cheek. 'We've got to go now and pick up the children, and I've got to get back to work. You take care of yourself and Marnie. I'll see you soon. Love you.'

He watched her go, her words echoing in his head.

She disappeared from view, and he closed his eyes and breathed in deeply, suddenly swamped by emotion.

I love you, too, Annie Brooks. I love you, too, and there's not a damn thing I can do about it...

CHAPTER NINE

OVER THE NEXT few days, things settled down.

Ed's grief receded, Marnie seemed to be coping, and work was as busy as ever. But there was still the question of Annie.

He'd used Marnie as an excuse to create a little distance between them outside work, but in their working hours they were thrown together constantly and it was killing him.

Like now. There she was, stripping off her gloves and plastic apron, heading towards him with a smile. He knew what she was going to say—

'Coffee? Before that blasted phone rings again?'

He hesitated for a heartbeat, and gave in.

'Coffee sounds great,' he said, and lobbing his gloves and apron into the bin he held the door of Resus open for her.

'So how are things?' she asked as they followed the path round to the café.

'OK, I think. She seems to be coping.'

'So my mother said. She and Marnie are taking the girls to the beach hut today. I was asking about you.'

'Me? I'm fine.'

Apart from losing my best friend and cutting myself off from the only woman I've ever loved.

She gave him a frankly disbelieving look, but they were in the queue for coffee and not even Annie would challenge him in those circumstances.

He added a blueberry muffin and a banana to the coffees, paid the bill and ushered her out.

'Well, here we are again,' she said, settling onto the bench he'd come to think of as theirs. 'So, how are you, really?'

He shrugged. 'Actually, I am all right. I miss him, but I've missed him for years. We lost him about three years ago in terms of his personality. More, maybe. It was just very sudden at the end, but then I'm not sure you're ever really ready to say goodbye.'

He looked at her, scanned her face and wondered how, when he left—which he would do—he'd ever say goodbye to her. He'd do it, because he had to, but he'd never be ready. Not if he lived to be a hundred.

'What are you doing this evening?' she asked, changing the subject out of the blue.

'Why?'

She gave him a slow, understanding smile. 'I thought it would be nice for us to spend some time together, take your mind off things a bit. I could cook for us.'

'At your house?'

'No. At yours.'

He was tempted. He knew how it would end up, though, with them tangled in his bedding, gasping for breath and waiting for the aftershocks to fade away before they started again. He looked away, afraid his eyes would give him away. His body was certainly having a good go.

'I ought to see Marnie.'

'Really?'

No, not really. He hadn't planned to see her, and she'd made it quite clear that she was happy spending time alone going through Ned's things and remembering the good times. But—Annie?

'Annie, this isn't going anywhere,' he said heavily.

Her smile was tender and made him want to haul her into his arms and hold her tight. 'I know that. I'm being selfish. I want to spend time with you while I can.'

Selfish? Not his Annie. She was trying to look after him, make sure he ate, make sure he wasn't falling into depression. Which he wasn't. He just wanted her, and he couldn't have her, and she was making it impossibly difficult to walk away cleanly. *And she wasn't his Annie!*

'No.'

The word seemed to tear a hole in him, but it had to be said. He had to stop this thing right here, right now, before it destroyed him.

There was a heartbeat of silence before she spoke, and then her voice was quiet and matter-of-fact. 'No, as in not tonight, or, no, as in never again?'

He forced himself to turn his head and look her in the eye. It was the least she deserved after her unstinting support of the past two and a half weeks. More.

'No as in never again,' he said firmly. 'I'm sorry. We're getting in too deep, Annie, and we're both going to get hurt.'

Hell, what was he talking about? They were already hurting, but it was too late to turn the clock back. The damage was done.

She held his eyes steadily. 'We don't have to get hurt. It doesn't have to be goodbye.'

'No! There's no way we're doing this. No way I'm going to let you end up in the same position as Marnie—'

'Have you spoken to her about it?' she asked calmly, as if her world wasn't falling apart around her ears. 'Asked her how she feels? Because she wouldn't change a minute of their lives together.'

He turned his head away. He couldn't look at her, couldn't see the love there, just waiting for him to say the word. It was ripping him apart.

'We aren't them. They didn't have a choice. She didn't know.'

'And if she had? If they'd known they both

carried the gene? They still would have married. They might not have had children, but they still would have married and shared their lives together right to the end, because they loved each other. And you know that's true. And, anyway, it's only speculation. You might not get it.'

His chest felt tight, and suddenly he couldn't breathe. 'I don't want to talk about this here,' he said abruptly. 'We're at work. I can't do it.'

He got up and walked away, his coffee barely touched, the muffin and banana lying on the bench beside her.

She finished her coffee slowly, picked up his food and took it and the coffee in to him. He was working at the desk, and she put them down beside him.

'Here. You left these behind.'

And without saying another word, she walked off and tackled the next patient in the queue.

The next few days were strained.

Thursday was better, because he was off, and from Friday to Sunday she was off, too.

And on the Saturday evening, three weeks to

the day after his grandfather had died, she realised her period was late.

Almost a week late. And she was never late. Ever. Well, only once.

She made an excuse to her mother about needing some fresh air, went out to the supermarket, bought a test and phoned Ed.

'Are you at home?'

'No. Why?'

'I need to talk to you.'

'Can it wait till Monday?'

'No. It can't.'

She heard him sigh. 'I'm at Marnie's, doing some gardening. Come now, meet me at the beach hut.'

She drove to the car park on the cliff, walked down the steps and arrived at the beach hut just as he did. He was sweaty, dirty, covered in tiny bits of grass, and it was obviously the last place he wanted to be.

'Will this take long?'

She glanced at the hut, still locked as if he didn't want to open the Pandora's box of memories it contained. The night he'd made love to her. The night his grandfather had died and she'd stood and held him for almost an hour in silence.

'Not necessarily. My period's late.'

He went chalk-white and grabbed the metal railings, bracing himself against them as if he'd been punched in the gut. She could hear the rasp of his breath, see the heaving of his shoulders as he struggled to take in the implications. And then finally he straightened and stared out to sea, his face a rigid mask.

'How late?'

'Five days. And I'm never late.'

He swore savagely under his breath and turned to face her, his eyes tortured. 'This can't happen, Annie. It can't. The risk—'

'You don't even know if there is a risk.'

He sucked in his breath and recoiled, but he didn't answer. How could he? Without getting the test results, he had no idea if he'd passed on this awful gene to the child she might be carrying. Even the thought made him want to weep for it.

Had the gene expanded? Did he even carry it?

He didn't know, and, dammit, he didn't *want* to know, but if she was pregnant—

'Have you done a pregnancy test?'

'No. I've bought one. I've got it with me.'

'Do it now. There are loos just along here.'

She followed him, and he stood outside, arms folded, heart pounding, while she went into the cubicle and closed the door. She came out a few moments later with a white wand in her hand, and they stood together and watched it.

One line.

Just one.

They waited, and waited, but there was no change, and he felt the tension leave him like the air from a punctured balloon.

'You're not pregnant.' His voice sounded hollow to his ears, distorted by the pounding of his heart. He waited for the relief to kick in, but for some reason it didn't.

'I didn't get a positive test last time until I was two weeks late. Positive means you're pregnant. Negative doesn't mean you aren't, it means pregnancy hormones haven't been detected, but that could be because I'm not pregnant, or because the hormone levels aren't yet high enough.'

'But it could mean you aren't pregnant. You might not be.'

'No. I might not be. But I might be. And if I am, before you even ask the question, I'm having it, and I'm not having amniocentesis either. It's too risky and it won't change how I feel.'

'No, this is our baby, it's not just down to you,' he said, feeling backed into a corner of a room he'd never wanted to enter.

'I think you'll find in law it is.'

He stared at her for a second, letting her words sink in, letting it all sink in. The ramifications of it were enormous, and as it hit him, he let out a shaky breath and shook his head.

'Annie, why are we even talking about the law?' he asked desperately. 'This could be our child—'

He wasn't sure who moved first, but she was in his arms, wrapped hard against his chest, her shoulders shaking as she gave in to her fears, and all he could think was, *How? How can she be pregnant? How could I have been so careless? When?*

There was only one possible time, when he'd been so desperate, so distracted that he might have forgotten. The night before his grandfather had died.

His arms tightened convulsively. 'I'm so sorry. This is all my fault.'

'It's nobody's fault.'

'Yes, it is. I forgot—the night before he died, in the night. I forgot.'

'So did I. It takes two, Ed. I'm not going to let you martyr yourself over this so don't even think about it.'

She pushed away and looked up into his face. 'You're disgustingly sweaty, do you know that?' she said, but she was smiling tenderly and she lifted a hand and wiped the dirt from his cheek as if he was a grubby child, and he turned his head and pressed his lips to her palm.

'I'm really sorry.'

'About the sweat?'

'About not protecting you. About the baby.'

'We don't know yet if there is one.'

'No. We don't.' He tilted back his head and let out a sigh, and she rested her head back on his sweaty chest and hugged him.

'Why don't we cross one bridge at a time?' she suggested softly, and he nodded.

'OK, but in the meantime be careful what you eat. No caffeine, no soft cheese or prawns, no unpasteurised milk products—'

'No alcohol, no drugs. I do remember.'

'Are you feeling sick?'

'A bit, but that's probably worry.'

'Have you eaten?'

'Yes. Have you?'

He nodded. 'Look, why don't I go back to Marnie's and put the tools away and meet you back at my house?'

'What for? Until we have an answer, this doesn't change anything,' she pointed out, but his defences were breached, and he wanted her. He wanted to hold her, and talk about the future, and plan for a baby they should never have conceived and who might not even exist—

He dropped his arms and moved away a fraction, distancing himself to make it easier. 'No.

You're right. Well—I'll see you on Monday, then. Let me know if there's any change.'

They checked the wand again, but there was still only the one blue line, and it took him a moment to realise that the feeling washing over him was disappointment.

He took another step back, literally and metaphorically. 'I need to go. Where are you parked?'

'At the top.'

He nodded, and they walked back together in tense silence. He paused beside her car, waiting till she was behind the wheel.

'I'll see you on Monday,' he repeated, and closing the door for her he turned on his heel and walked away.

She wasn't pregnant.

Or, at least, not any more. She woke on Sunday morning with cramping pain, and by lunchtime she was bleeding heavily.

An early miscarriage? It could be. She never had problem periods. Four days, max, of nothing untoward. Not like this.

Her mother found her sitting on the edge of her bed in tears, and just hugged her.

'Want to talk about it?'

She shook her head. What could she say to her? I think I'm having a miscarriage? She hadn't even had a positive pregnancy test. It could just be a period.

'Go and wash your face and freshen up. I'll make you a cup of tea,' her mother said.

She went into the bathroom, dithered for a moment and then tried the second test in the packet, convinced it would still be negative, and it showed a faint, very faint second line.

She had been pregnant. Had been. Past tense. It was just the circulating hormones still in her bloodstream. Or had she had a threatened miscarriage, and the baby might still be clinging on? A little glimmer of hope dawned, but by nine that evening, she was sure she'd miscarried. She'd had clots, heavy bleeding and cramping pain, and she felt a sense of utter desolation.

Oh, well, at least Ed would be pleased. Not to mention ecstatic.

She'd tell him in the morning, but for now all she wanted to do was curl up in a ball and howl her eyes out.

* * *

He didn't sleep that night, or the following night.

He was too busy thinking, all the available options going round and round in his head—but there was only one option truly open to him, because if she was pregnant he couldn't bear the suspense for the next eighteen or more years until his own son or daughter was old enough to be allowed to take the test.

An unborn foetus could be tested, and Annie had said no.

But what if the child never wanted the answer? What if it was a case of waiting for the onset of HD, either in him or in his child? He would be on tenterhooks for years, until either he or his child showed symptoms.

For the first time he had an insight into what Marnie and his brother were going through with him, and he felt sick.

No. If Annie was pregnant, there was only one option open to him, one he'd been avoiding for years.

He had to get the test results. Annie had been right when she'd accused him of running from the truth. He was. He was trying to outrun reality, and it might just have caught up with him.

It hadn't. He walked into the department on Monday morning and bumped into Annie. She was waiting for him, her face pale, her eyes red-rimmed.

'Good news,' she said, but her smile was wobbly and her eyes suddenly glazed and she turned away and walked off.

He ran after her, catching her arm and turning her back to face him. 'Talk to me. What's happened?'

'Do you really need me to spell it out for you?' she said sarcastically, and tugged her arm to free it.

He let her go, his heart heavy. Damn. Oddly, it didn't feel like good news, and judging by the look on her face it hadn't been good news for her either.

She'd wanted to have his child—dammit, he'd wanted her to have his child, and she wasn't going to. No baby to look forward to, no reason to be with her, to stay with her and marry her and have it all. Nothing. Because she wasn't pregnant after all, and just like that the dream had just slipped through his fingers like sand.

The realisation of all he'd lost, all he'd been hoping for, hit him like a brick wall and he had to remind himself to breathe.

God, he hadn't even realised how much he'd wanted it—

'Ed? Annie's not feeling great. I think you should come.'

It was Kate, and he followed her swiftly down the corridor to the little staffroom he hardly ever used. She was in there, curled up on a chair, arms wrapped round her abdomen, rocking gently.

'I'll deal with it,' he said, and he shooed Kate out and closed the door and sat down beside her.

'Annie?'

'I'm all right,' she said, but she was as white as a sheet and he knew she wasn't.

'That's bull. What's going on? You look awful.'

She lifted her tear-stained face and met his eyes. 'I'm having a miscarriage,' she said brokenly. 'I had a positive test yesterday, very faint. And I was bleeding heavily. I still am.'

Oh, dear God.

Her face crumpled, and he wrapped her gently in his arms and cradled her against his side, and she sobbed as if her heart was broken.

Maybe it was. His own felt torn in two, one half relieved, the other devastated at the loss of a child he'd never even known they'd conceived. Not *known*. Suspected, but not known. And he'd thought he hadn't wanted it. Worse, he'd let her think he hadn't wanted it.

Guilt, remorse and grief swamped him, and he squeezed his eyes shut tight against the sting of tears. 'You shouldn't be here, you need to go home. Is your mother there?'

She nodded.

'Good. I'll check you over and make sure you don't need admitting and then I'll take you home. We're quiet at the moment. I'll find a side room and do a scan and some obs. Come on.'

He helped her to her feet and steered her to an empty room and checked her over, but she was fine.

There was no sign of a foetus that he could see, although it was a bit early to tell, but there wasn't an ectopic pregnancy, which had been his main worry. And her blood pressure and oxygen saturation were fine.

He took her home, left her with her mother and went back to work to face a barrage of questions.

'She's just under the weather,' he said, flatly refusing to discuss it with the others, and threw himself back into work.

The GP came, at her mother's insistence, and she was signed off for the rest of the week.

It wasn't really necessary, not physically, but emotionally she felt as if she'd gone through the wringer.

Or a bereavement?

But it wasn't just her baby she'd lost, it was Ed's baby, and with it Ed himself, because without the baby to tie him to her, they'd have no need to stay in touch.

He sent her flowers. They arrived on Monday afternoon, and they made her cry. The card just said, 'I'm sorry.'

Was he? She didn't know, and they didn't seem to be talking, so it was hard to be sure.

He rang her that evening, though, to ask how

she was, and said Kate sent her love, but it was a very brief call and he didn't really say anything. There was nothing to say, was there?

Tuesday was more of the same, except that she was feeling better. By Wednesday evening she was fine, apart from a crazy tendency to burst into tears.

'Are you OK if I go for a walk?' she asked her mother. 'I'm going nuts.'

'Of course. Will you be all right?'

'I'm fine. I just need to get out and stretch my legs and get some air.'

'Take your phone and don't go too far. Call me if you need me.'

'Oh, Mum. I love you.'

Her mother hugged her gently. 'I love you, too. Take care.'

What harm could come to her that hadn't already? Not much. Her heart was already broken, her baby was gone, the man she loved had no reason to stay with her now—what else could possibly happen?

The blast of a horn made her jump and freeze in her tracks, just as a car swerved round her and left her shaking on the edge of the kerb, stunned. What was she doing? Crossing without looking? Without even being aware? She didn't even know where she was.

She heard running footsteps, and someone grabbed her arms.

'Christ, Annie, I thought I was going to kill you—what were you doing? Are you all right? Did I hit you?'

Ed. It was Ed, driving home from work probably, or from Marnie's. She closed her eyes and felt the tears slide down her cheeks as he hauled her against his chest and held her tight.

'I'm sorry. I wasn't looking.'

'Where were you going?'

'I don't know. A walk.'

He kept one arm round her back and ushered her forwards. 'Come on, get in the car, I'll drive you home. You're shaking all over.'

'No. Not home. Can we go to yours?'

'Sure.'

It was only a couple of roads away, but she probably wouldn't have made it because her legs were so wobbly with the shock. He put the car away, led her into the house and sat her down on the sofa.

'Are you OK? Are you sure I didn't hit you?'

'No, of course you didn't—'

'There was no of course about it! You were just about to step out into the road without looking!' His face paled. 'Hell, you weren't—'

'No, Ed, I wasn't trying to kill myself,' she said tiredly. 'I just wasn't paying attention. I'm sorry I scared you.'

'Scared me? You took years off my life!' He stabbed his hands through his hair and let out his breath on a sharp sigh. 'God, woman, you need a keeper.'

She tilted her head back and threw him a wry glance. 'Are you volunteering?'

The silence was complete, broken only by the ticking of the clock on the mantelpiece and her words, hanging in the air.

Was he?

He sat down next to her as if his strings had been cut.

'Hey, don't look so panic-stricken, I was joking.'

He looked at her. Really looked at her. She wasn't joking. And neither was he.

And that scared him, more than her stepping off the kerb, more than the threat of HD hanging over him. There was no way they were going to end up together while that threat was still there, now there was no baby. He fought down the regret and said the first thing that came into his head.

'Good, because there's no way it's happening, especially now there's no need for it. And I'm really sorry I got you in this mess, but maybe it's just as well it's ended this way.'

She stiffened.

'Just as well? For who? For you, maybe.'

'No! For the child. It could have inherited HD—'

'Well, we'll never know, will we?' she said rawly. 'We don't even know if it was a possibility, but tell me this. If you had the gene, if you were to get onset of the symptoms now, would you wish you hadn't been born? Has your life been so meaningless, so unfulfilled that there's been no point to it?'

He frowned. 'No, of course not, but my parents didn't know there was a risk. We know! And it was criminally irresponsible of me not to make sure that you couldn't conceive my child, that I couldn't hand that defective gene on. Annie, HD is devastating—'

'I know that, but it's not unique! Cancer is devastating. Heart disease is devastating. Renal failure is devastating. That doesn't mean you kill all the embryos that might develop them! A shortened life doesn't mean it's worthless.'

'I never said it was, and I never suggested for a moment that you should kill our baby or harm it in any way. I just would never be able to forgive myself if it turned out that I'd passed it on.'

She sighed and sagged back against the sofa, too wrung out to deal with him and his endless denial. 'Ed, you don't even know if you have the damn HD gene so this entire conversation is pointless. Can you please take me home? I'm too tired to talk about this now and, anyway, there's nothing to talk about. Not any more.'

Tears welled in her eyes, and he sighed softly and got to his feet.

'I'm sorry. Of course I'll take you home. Come on.'

He led her out to the car, drove her home and then went back, opened a bottle of wine and sat in the garden.

Was she right? Were they all right? His entire life was being driven by a hypothesis based on speculation. And if he only had the courage to do it, he could find out the answer.

One thing was for sure. He wouldn't find it in the bottom of a bottle. He poured it away, cleared up the kitchen and went to bed.

CHAPTER TEN

HE RANG HER the following morning.

'Can we talk?'

She sighed softly. She really, really didn't want to do this again. She still felt raw, reamed out inside from so much loss, and, anyway, where was it all going? Nowhere. 'Is there anything new to say?'

'Yes, there is. Are you busy?'

She looked across the garden to the little play-house where the girls were happily 'cooking' on their toy stove. Her mother was hanging washing on the line, and she turned to Annie.

'Go,' she said quietly. 'I'm fine with the girls. Go and talk to him.'

She wasn't at all sure she wanted to, but he seemed to have something he wanted to say to her. Maybe—

No. She crushed the little flicker of hope.

'OK. Shall I come round?'

'No, I'll pick you up in ten minutes.'

He hung up, and she stared at the phone in annoyance. Autocratic—

'He's coming in ten minutes. I suppose I ought to change.'

'Well, unless you're going out in your pyjamas.'

She gave a hollow little laugh and took herself off for the fastest shower on record. Her hair was fine, she'd washed it last night while she'd stood in the shower and cried with frustration.

Jeans, she thought. Jeans and a linen top. Loose and comfortable and pretty. Not that pretty mattered. She was done trying to appeal to Ed Shackleton.

There was no time for fancy make-up. She put on a spritz of perfume, a quick flick of mascara and some concealer under her eyes, a touch of lipgloss and she was good to go.

He was waiting outside with the lid down, propped on the side of the car with his ankles crossed and his arms folded. He had a soft cotton shirt on with jeans, and a navy sweater slung over his shoulders, the arms tied loosely round his neck. He looked good enough to eat, and she despised herself for being so easily impressed.

He wasn't smiling, though. He pushed himself away from the car and walked towards her slowly, shoving his hands in his pockets. 'Hi. How are you?'

'I'm all right. I've been better.'

He frowned, and nodded slightly in acknowledgement. 'Do you need a sweater?'

'I don't know. Do I? Where are we going?'

'I'm not sure. Maybe Cambridge.'

'Cambridge?'

'It all depends.' He didn't say on what, but she sensed it was important so she went back inside, asked her mother if she'd be all right for the rest of the day with the girls, picked up a jumper and went back out.

'OK, I'm all yours.'

'Right, let's go for coffee.'

Coffee? She'd thought they were going to Cambridge? Apparently not, or not yet. He opened the door for her, shut it after she was in and slid behind the wheel.

They drove down to the new restaurant that had opened on the front, the one her mother and Marnie had gone to, and sat outside at one of the tables overlooking the sea.

'Lovely day again. Have you had breakfast?'

'Cereal, but I can always eat cake, if that's what you're asking.'

He smiled for the first time, ordered two cappuccinos and a slice each of the carrot and lemon drizzle cakes because she couldn't decide, and then propped his elbows on the table and frowned down at his hands. His fingers were linked, and he was moving them restlessly, as if he was trying to work out what to say and didn't know where to start.

'Ed, spit it out.'

He dropped his hands, sat back and gave a wry laugh. 'Is it so obvious?'

'Well, you rang and said you wanted to talk. I assumed you didn't just want to talk about the weather and my breakfast.'

'No.' His smile wry, he glanced around, but they were alone.

Neutral territory, she realised with a moment of insight.

'OK. If you were still pregnant—if you hadn't—'

He broke off, unable to say it, but she finished the sentence for him.

'If I hadn't lost the baby?' She gave a fractured little laugh and looked out to sea. 'Lost,' she said idly. 'What kind of a word is that? It makes it sound so careless, as if I didn't look after it. Mislaid it somewhere.' She looked back at him and glimpsed a fleeting pain in the back of his eyes, quickly masked. 'So, anyway, if I hadn't "lost" the baby, what?'

He frowned, his brows crunching briefly together. 'If you hadn't, if you were still pregnant, how would you see this panning out?'

She gave another desperate little laugh and looked up at him. 'I have no idea. Us together, making a home and a family with my girls and our little one? Hardly. It's way too unlikely and we both know it wasn't going to happen. You've got your life to live, and you're determined to do it your way, and now there's nothing stopping you.'

Nothing, he thought, except the fact that he loved her much, much more than he would have dreamed possible. Much more than he loved anyone else in the world, himself included. Next to hers, his own needs paled into insignificance. And because of that, he threw a little more honesty into the mix.

'When I thought you might be pregnant, I decided that if you found you were, I'd make an appointment with the genetic counsellor.'

She stared at him. 'Really?'

'Yes. Really. I decided that if you were going to have my child, I had to know if I'd inherited that defective gene, and whether or not it had expanded, whether or not I might have handed on a time bomb to my child. I realised I couldn't live the rest of my life in suspense, just waiting for the other shoe to drop. It wasn't fair on you, on the child, on me.'

She nodded slowly, then her mouth twisted into a sad little smile. 'Well, you don't have to worry about it now.'

'No. I don't. Except I think maybe I do. It made me realise what Marnie feels about me, and what my brother feels. That horrible suspense, the thing hanging over them. I've been ignoring it for years, blanking it out, running away from it, but they couldn't blank it out and ignore it because they felt guilty, my brother because he hasn't inherited it, and Marnie because she might have been responsible for handing it on to me through my father. And I don't want them to feel like that any longer.'

'Wow. That's quite a decision. So are you going to ask for the result?'

'Yes. I think so. I'm sick of running. I want to know, now. I didn't think it affected my future, I hadn't let myself think about it, but of course it does, and it could change everything.' Including his relationship with her, but he didn't want to raise that until he knew, one way or the other. 'I need to know.'

Her eyes didn't waver, but she nodded slowly. 'And when you get your result, if you have the faulty gene, if it's expanded, will you tell them then? Your family?'

He frowned down at his hands. Stupidly, he hadn't thought of that. 'I don't know. Depends how bad it is. How many repeats.' He gave a hollow laugh. 'I'm doing it partly because Marnie wants reassurance, but it hadn't even occurred to me I might just make it worse for her.'

She leant forward, concerned for him even though she felt so battered by his decision-making process and the effect it had had on their relationship. 'You don't have to do it, you do know that, don't you? Not for me, not for them, not for anyone but yourself. It has to come from you.'

He nodded. 'It is coming from me. This time.'

'So are you going to make an appointment?'

'I've got one. They had a cancellation at two this afternoon, in Cambridge. That's why I'm going.'

Wow. He really intended to do it. No wonder he looked so tense. 'Do you want me to come with you?'

He met her eyes searchingly. 'Would you?'

'If you want me to, of course I will.'

'Two cappuccinos, lemon drizzle and carrot cake?'

She leant back, smiled at the waiter and waited for him to leave before going on.

'I don't have to come in with you. I can wait outside, or in the car. Whatever. Your call.'

He nodded. He clearly hadn't made up his mind yet about that, but that was fine. If she went with him, he had the option. If she didn't go with him, he didn't.

'Come with me,' he said finally, and she nodded and pushed the cakes towards him.

'Want to have half and half?'

And at last he smiled.

They travelled cross-country, on the back roads. It took longer, but they had plenty of time and it was a gorgeous day. The roof was down, their hair was blowing in the wind, and tootling along through the country lanes with the birds singing overhead in the branches was strangely calming.

But by the time they got to Cambridge, he still didn't know if he wanted her with him when he got the results.

They hadn't talked about it on the way, by tacit agreement. They hadn't talked about anything much. Marnie, mostly, and the fact that she wanted to sell the house and downsize.

He was gutted by that because he loved the house and it held so many wonderful memories for him, but it was her decision. Just as this was his.

He found a space in the hospital car park, by a miracle, and they went and found a café and bought some sandwiches and picked at them.

'You should eat,' he said to her, but maybe she was nervous, too. He knew he was. His stomach was in knots, and he still wasn't sure he had the guts to go through with it.

'What are you going to ask? Do you want to know all of it, or just if you have the defective gene or not?'

His heart beat a little tattoo against his ribs and he abandoned the sandwich. 'I don't know.'

'What's the bottom line for you?'

'Has it expanded.'

'Changed the level of risk to you, in other words? OK. So maybe ask that first?'

He nodded. 'If the answer's yes, do I want to know how much?'

'I don't know. I can't advise you, Ed, and I won't. This is too big a thing for me to be influencing you.'

'But you are influencing me. If it wasn't for you, I wouldn't be here.'

'But I didn't ask you to do this.'

'Did you want to?'

She smiled sadly at him. 'Oh, Ed.' She took his hand, folding it between hers, squeezing it tight as she let go of her own fears and gave him the truth.

'Of course I want to know, but I'm not going to ask you to do this against your better judgement. It's a tough thing to do, I know that, and you have to be utterly sure you want the answer, whatever it turns out to be, because you can't just hand it back if you don't like it. So by all means do it for yourself, but don't do it for me, because it won't change how I feel.'

'It should.'

'No, it shouldn't,' she said, and laid all her cards on the table. 'Look, I don't know what's happening with us, I don't know what you feel about me, where you want to take it, but no matter where we go with this, if we have a future or not, this result won't change the fact that I love you, and I'll love you for ever, whatever happens to you, or to us.

'It might influence our decisions. We might not want to have children, or we might want to go the IVF route and screen the embryos. Or there's all the other possibilities like gene silencing and things like that being developed that could totally change the prognosis in the future. But whatever we decided to do about that, whatever happens to you, I want to be there, by your side, because I love you and I think you love me. So there you have it. What happens next is down to you.'

His fingers tightened on hers, his eyes intense, searching. 'You don't know what you're saying.'

'Of course I do. I'm a doctor. I'm well aware. I've listened to you talking about your grandfather, I've listened to Marnie, I've done research, I've seen patients with it—Ed, I *know* what I'm saying. And I mean every single word of it.'

His eyes scanned hers again, his face a mask,

and then he nodded. She could see a pulse beating in his neck, feel the tension radiating off him.

'Will you wait here for me?'

'Of course I'll wait. You don't have to ask. There's just one thing. Can I have a hug, please, before you go?'

'Oh, Annie—'

He scooped her up, wrapped his arms around her and rocked her gently against his heart. He could have stayed there for ever, putting off the evil moment, absorbing the strength of this incredible woman who apparently loved him enough to do this for him, but time was ticking on and he let her go reluctantly.

'I'll see you as soon as I'm done. Have you got your phone?'

'Yes.'

'I'll call you as soon as I'm done.'

He kissed her, a hard, desperate kiss loaded with emotion, and then he dropped his arms and strode away. She waited until he was out of sight, then sat down again abruptly. She needed a cold drink, some fresh air and an end to this.

Well, she could manage the cold drink and the fresh air. The rest would have to wait.

His head was reeling.

Reeling with facts and figures, bottom lines and possibilities, not all of them good. But not bad.

He pulled out his phone and called Annie, and she answered instantly, as if she'd been sitting waiting with the phone in her hand.

'Hi. I'm done. Where are you?'

'Where you left me. I've just got a bottle of water.'

'Bring it with you. Meet me at the car.'

She was there before him, and he let her into the car and slid in beside her.

'Well?'

'Not here.'

He drove out into the country, parked the car in a field entrance and propped his hands on the wheel. Beside him Annie was rigid with tension, her hands locked together, the knuckles white.

'OK, bottom line. I've got the gene, but it didn't expand when my father handed it down to me.'

'You won't get it?'

'No. I won't get it. Ever.'

There was a strangled sob from beside him, and he turned and caught her as she threw herself into his arms and hung on tight.

'Oh, thank God,' she said raggedly. 'I didn't know what you were going to say. I thought—oh, I don't know what I thought. I knew it wasn't totally good news when I saw you, but I didn't know how bad it might be. Oh, Ed, I'm so glad you're safe. I thought…' She pushed him away and lifted her hand. He felt her fingers on his face, wiping away tears—his?—with infinite tenderness.

'Are you OK?' she asked softly.

He nodded. 'Yeah. Yeah, I'm OK. It could have been a lot, lot worse.'

'It could. Tell Marnie, she needs to know.'

'No. I'll go and tell her, face to face. If I didn't have the gene, I'd call her, but although it's good news for me, this isn't really what she wanted to hear so I need to tell her gently because it still has repercussions.' He let out a soft sigh. 'God, I feel wrung out. Have you got that water?'

She handed it to him, and he drank half of it, handed the bottle back and started the car. She took the cap off again and sipped it, watching him out of the corner of her eye.

He seemed happier. Freer, somehow, as if a huge weight had been taken off him. Had he even realised he'd been carrying it around for so many years?

She put the cap back on the water, rested her head back and closed her eyes. She felt drained after the past few traumatic days, and the sun on her face, the birds in the trees and the gentle breeze lulled her off to sleep.

'Hey, sleepyhead.'

She woke with a start, and looked around. 'Oh. We're at mine.'

'I thought your girls might want to see you today.' He hesitated for a moment. 'What are you doing later?'

'Nothing.'

'Can your mother babysit?'

'Again?'

'Please? Pretty please with a cherry on top?'

She laughed softly. 'I expect so. I'll let you know.'

'Good. I'll see you later.'

He let her out of the car, kissed her lightly on the cheek and watched her let herself in, and then, taking a long, deep breath, he put the car in gear and drove to Marnie's.

She was in the garden, pottering quietly in the greenhouse with a rubbish bag and the compost bin. 'I'm having a clear-out,' she said. 'It's such a mess in here. Ned would be so annoyed if he could see it.'

'Come out,' he said, taking the pots out of her hand and putting them down on the wooden staging. 'I've got something to tell you.'

'What? Have you finally come to your senses and proposed to that nice girl?'

He laughed. 'Yes and no. Come on, sit down. We need to talk.'

'Gosh, it sounds serious.'

'It is serious. I went to get my test result.'

Her hand flew to her mouth, and she stifled a gasp. 'Oh, Ed. And?'

'Same as Dad. Same as you. I'll be fine, but

I won't have children because of the risk.' The words seemed to sear through him, and he sucked in a breath.

'Oh, darling. I was so hoping—'

'Marnie, I'm fine. I'll be all right. That's all that matters. I just won't risk passing it on.'

Her eyes welled. 'Oh, that's such a shame. You'd be a brilliant father. Are you all right about it?'

He shrugged. 'Sort of gutted about not having my own kids, but—no, it's good. It means I can make informed decisions about what I want to do with my life instead of just running away.'

'Have you told Annie?'

He nodded. 'She was with me. Not when I got the results, but she went with me in the car.'

'So what prompted this?'

'Annie did,' he said, feeling a wave of sadness. 'She had a miscarriage at the weekend. She was only a few days overdue, hadn't even had a positive pregnancy test till the day it happened. She's been off work all week.'

She tsked softly and reached over to squeeze his hand. 'Oh, darling, I'm so sorry.'

'So am I. I'm relieved that I haven't passed on the HD gene, but I'm gutted about the baby. It made me realise—well, all sorts of things.'

'So what happens now?'

'Now?' His phone rang and he answered it. 'Hi, Annie. Can she do it?'

'Yes. What time?'

'After the girls are in bed?'

'Half-past seven?'

'Sounds good. Wear the long blue dress. And don't eat first.'

'Oh! OK. I'll see you later.'

'See you later. Bye.'

He slipped his phone back into his pocket and smiled at Marnie. 'Now I'm going to take her out for dinner.'

'Somewhere nice?'

'Somewhere very nice.'

'Good. It's about time. Let me know what she says.'

'About?'

Marnie just smiled at him and shook her head patiently. 'Go on, shoo. I've got to clear up this lot. I've got an estate agent coming round tomorrow.'

'What?'

'You heard.'

'No. Stop. Do nothing. Get it valued, but do nothing else.'

'Why?'

'Because rumour has it there's a paediatric consultancy coming up in Yoxburgh and if Annie—well, I might want to buy it from you.'

Her eyes filled with tears and she flung her arms around him. 'Oh, you dear, sweet, sentimental boy…'

'I'm hardly any of those things, Marnie, and, anyway, it's a sound investment.'

She let him go and tapped him on the nose. 'Don't lie to your grandmother. You know perfectly well I can see straight through you. Now go and get yourself ready for this evening, and shave, would you? You look a mess. And before you go, I've got something for you.'

He picked her up on the dot of seven-thirty and took her to the restaurant where they'd had coffee that morning.

It seemed like a lifetime ago.

They sat inside this time, watching the sun set over the sea, and it was wonderful.

The food was wonderful, the atmosphere was wonderful, the service was wonderful—and she wasn't sure why they were there. She'd thought, maybe…but that was just a foolish hope, and she should have known better.

'Let's not bother with coffee,' he said, and summoned the waiter with a flick of his eyebrow.

He paid the bill, left a hefty tip and ushered her out, and to her surprise he went the wrong way.

'Why are we going this way?'

'I've got a surprise for you.'

'Oh.'

Her heart hiccupped, and when he pulled up in the cliff-top car park and let her down the steps, she was puzzled.

He was taking her to the beach hut? Why?

She soon found out.

'Wait here,' he said, and moments later he opened the doors wide and beckoned her in.

The inside was lit by what seemed like a thousand tea lights, flickering in glass holders all around the sides, and she could see champagne cooling in the ice bucket on the table, with strawberries and dainty cocoa-dusted truffles next to it in a pretty little bonbon dish.

He sat her down, and she thought he was about to open the champagne, but instead he picked up the bonbon dish and offered it to her.

'Thank you— Oh!'

Nestled in the middle, resting on a dark chocolate truffle, was a ring. It was nothing flashy, just a pretty diamond solitaire set in platinum, and she stared at it, a little stunned, not quite sure what to do.

'I don't know,' he said quietly, 'if you've meant everything you've said to me in the last twenty-four hours about loving me and the result not making any difference, so if you didn't mean it, now would be a good time to say so.'

She looked up at him and his mouth flickered in a smile, but his eyes were expressionless and there was a muscle working in his jaw.

'Of course I meant it.'

'Thank God for that,' he said under his breath, and before she could react, he went down on one knee in front of her, took the ring out of the truffles and took her hand in his.

'I love you, Annie. I've been fighting it like I seem to fight everything, trying to outrun it, but I can't, and I realised this week that I didn't want to. I realised when you told me about the baby that I wanted it all—you, the girls, our baby, the happy ever after—all of it. And we were so close to having it, and it made me realise I couldn't let it slip away, but I could only have it on my terms.

'That was why I wouldn't let you come with me for the results, in case it was bad news, to give me time to get my defences up. If I'd been going to get HD, I would have walked away from you—'

'Maybe I wouldn't have let you.'

He frowned. 'You really are a fighter, aren't you?'

'I am for what I know is right, and for what I love. And I love you. And if you're down there on the floor volunteering to be my keeper after all this, the answer's yes.'

He laughed softly. 'Would you let me do this properly?'

She smiled at him lovingly. 'Only if you get on with it. I'm dying of suspense.'

He tutted, took her hand again and looked up into her eyes.

'Annie Brooks, you've brought light and hope and joy into my life, and I love you. I can't give you children, or at least not in the easy way, and maybe not at all, but I can and will give you my love, my heart, my soul, for as long as I'm alive. Will you do me the honour of consenting to be my wife?'

She was going to tease him again, but her eyes were suddenly glazed with tears, and she bit her lip. 'Yes,' she said breathlessly, on a tiny sob of joy. 'Oh, yes, my love, of course I will. Of course I'll marry you.'

The ring was a perfect fit.

She glanced down at it, stroking it with a gentle finger. 'Where did this come from? It's beautiful.'

'It's Marnie's ring. My grandfather gave it to her fifty-six years ago when he asked her to marry him. She's worn it every day ever since, and she wanted you to have it. She said it was the right thing to do, and she hopes it'll bring us as much happiness as it brought them.'

'Oh, bless her heart.' She pressed her lips to it and tried to fight back the tears, but they fell anyway, and he gathered her up against his heart and held her tight.

'Oh, sorry, I feel such an idiot. Fancy crying—'

'Don't worry. I nearly cried when she gave it to me. So did she.'

He sat her down again, picked up the champagne bottle and popped the cork deftly. Vapour flowed softly over the beautiful crystal flutes as he poured the champagne, and he put the bottle back in the ice and handed one to her.

'To Marnie and Ned, an inspiration, and to us.'

'To Marnie and Ned, and to us,' she said, and she touched her glass to his.

* * * * *

October

200 HARLEY STREET: SURGEON IN A TUX	Carol Marinelli
200 HARLEY STREET: GIRL FROM THE RED CARPET	Scarlet Wilson
FLIRTING WITH THE SOCIALITE DOC	Melanie Milburne
HIS DIAMOND LIKE NO OTHER	Lucy Clark
THE LAST TEMPTATION OF DR DALTON	Robin Gianna
RESISTING HER REBEL HERO	Lucy Ryder

November

200 HARLEY STREET: THE PROUD ITALIAN	Alison Roberts
200 HARLEY STREET: AMERICAN SURGEON IN LONDON	Lynne Marshall
A MOTHER'S SECRET	Scarlet Wilson
RETURN OF DR MAGUIRE	Judy Campbell
SAVING HIS LITTLE MIRACLE	Jennifer Taylor
HEATHERDALE'S SHY NURSE	Abigail Gordon

December

200 HARLEY STREET: THE SOLDIER PRINCE	Kate Hardy
200 HARLEY STREET: THE ENIGMATIC SURGEON	Annie Claydon
A FATHER FOR HER BABY	Sue MacKay
THE MIDWIFE'S SON	Sue MacKay
BACK IN HER HUSBAND'S ARMS	Susanne Hampton
WEDDING AT SUNDAY CREEK	Leah Martyn

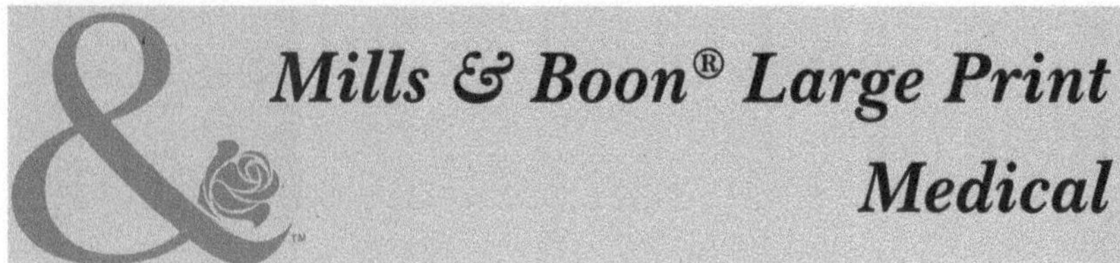

January

200 HARLEY STREET: THE SHAMELESS MAVERICK	Louisa George
200 HARLEY STREET: THE TORTURED HERO	Amy Andrews
A HOME FOR THE HOT-SHOT DOC	Dianne Drake
A DOCTOR'S CONFESSION	Dianne Drake
THE ACCIDENTAL DADDY	Meredith Webber
PREGNANT WITH THE SOLDIER'S SON	Amy Ruttan

February

TEMPTED BY HER BOSS	Scarlet Wilson
HIS GIRL FROM NOWHERE	Tina Beckett
FALLING FOR DR DIMITRIOU	Anne Fraser
RETURN OF DR IRRESISTIBLE	Amalie Berlin
DARING TO DATE HER BOSS	Joanna Neil
A DOCTOR TO HEAL HER HEART	Annie Claydon

March

A SECRET SHARED...	Marion Lennox
FLIRTING WITH THE DOC OF HER DREAMS	Janice Lynn
THE DOCTOR WHO MADE HER LOVE AGAIN	Susan Carlisle
THE MAVERICK WHO RULED HER HEART	Susan Carlisle
AFTER ONE FORBIDDEN NIGHT...	Amber McKenzie
DR PERFECT ON HER DOORSTEP	Lucy Clark

0914 LP 2B P2 Medical